# Praise for *Dark Crescent*

"It's a terrific collection of Scottish folktales with a modern twist, lyrical and evocative."
**Joanne Harris**

"Croal's *Dark Crescent* is a captivating constellation of folklore that feels both modern and ageless, deeply rooted and wonderfully original at the same time."
**Lorraine Wilson, author of *We Are All Ghosts in the Forest***

"A stunning collection of stories. A dark and delicious treat for fans of Scottish folklore. I delighted in discovering familiar (and sometimes not-so-familiar!) folklore creatures and stories told in Croal's unique, evocative style. The tales within are sometimes hopeful, usually dark, and always quickly devoured."
**Angie Spoto, author of *The Grief Nurse* and *The Bone Diver***

"With *Dark Crescent*, Lyndsey Croal invites readers into a world of darkness, magic, and the disturbing beauty of Scotland. Gorgeous and compelling!"
**Jonathan Maberry, NY Times bestselling author of *Burn to Shine* and *Mystic***

"Compelling and evocative, the stories of *Dark Crescent* shimmer with dark fairy tale magic. Highly recommended."
**Teika Marija Smits, author of *Umbilical* and *Waterlore***

# DARK CRESCENT

## Dark and seasonal tales from Scottish Folklore

## Lyndsey Croal

Text 2025 © Lyndsey Croal
Cover 2025 © Jenni Coutts
Section Illustrations 2025 © Cheney Hewitt
Bonus Section Illustrations 2025 © Lyndsey Croal
Harvester Logo 2019 © Francesca T Barbini

Editorial Team: Francesca T Barbini, Alex Davies, Cheney Hewitt
Typesetting: Francesca T Barbini, Cheney Hewitt

First published by Luna Press Publishing, Edinburgh, 2025



A CIP catalogue record is available from the British Library

www.lunapresspublishing.com

ISBN-13: 978-1-915556-57-8

REPRINTS:
'Nesting' in Dark Moon Digest Issue #44, and reprinted online with Crow & Cross Keys
'The Taxidermist' in Weird Tales Magazine
'Wisp in the Dark', in The Maul Magazine Issue One.
'Be Still, Iron Heart' in MYRIAD Zine Issue Two: Ironwood, and in *Bark & Bone*, from Space Cat Press.
'Woman of Ravens' in Quill & Crow Publishing's *The Crow's Quill: Covens*.
'Nuckelavee Winter' in British Fantasy Society Newsletter, and reprinted online in Wyldblood Magazine
'Two Faces of Winter' in Cunning Folk Magazine's *Spiritus Mundi* online.
'To Gut a Fish, First Gather its Bones' in Dark Matter INK's *Monster Lairs*
'The Lighthouse Seer' in Northern Gravy Issue Four
'The Woman of Thorns and the Honeycomb Queen' in Flame Tree Press Fantasy Con Newsletter and reprinted in Ellipsis Zine's *Wade*.
'The Loneliness of Water' in Hexagon Magazine Issue 12, and in *Shadows on the Water* from Flame Tree Press.
'A Kelpie's Breath' in Pen to Print's *Great Margin*.
'The Constellations of Daughter Death' in *Flash Fiction Online*.
'Seedseeker' in *Salt & Mirrors & Cats*.
'Last Call of the Deep' in *Shoreline of Infinity* Magazine Issue 30

*For content warnings, please see page 176*

*To Mum and Dad,
for first introducing me to the magic of other worlds.*

# Contents

# AUTUMN

# Dark Crescent

Two nights before I was destined to die for a second time, the omen was painted clear across the sky. Everything was still, save for the waves crackling on the grey pebbled beach. Then the humming began, distant and vague, as if heard through a shell. With it came a dark crescent, moving across the sky, twisting like a murmuring of starlings. It wasn't an ordinary flock, in that it wasn't made of birds, but of lost spirits dipping and diving in the gloaming. I watched for a moment, willing my fluttering heart to still. But I knew what it meant. Because I'd seen it once before.

~

Back home, Alasdair was setting a fire to ward off the cold. 'Clear sky tonight?'

'Yes,' I lied.

'It's funny,' he turned, face scrunched up in thought. 'I saw a flock of birds earlier, far from shore, all disoriented. They shouldn't be out after dark like that.'

My throat went dry. 'Must be the changing tides.'

He shrugged and returned to the fire. He didn't need to know that I'd seen them too. He wouldn't understand anyway if I explained what they meant. Off-islanders didn't believe the old tales. Besides, even if he did, he'd only try to intervene. And some things once set in motion can't be stopped. Ma taught me that.

'No surer things than omens,' she'd say.

~

The next morning, Alasdair headed to the shop, and I stayed to work on my latest commission: a seascape mosaic made from sea glass, broken pieces put together to make a whole. I'd finish it before the crescent returned. I didn't like leaving things incomplete.

I worked carefully, smoothing dull blues and greens into sparkling jewels from the deep. Giving them a new lease on life. Afterwards, I cleaned my studio and scrubbed under my fingernails until everything looked as good as new.

Alasdair made mussels for dinner. The smell of them wafted through the cottage and I inhaled the scent, savouring the earthiness.

'You spoil me,' I told him.

'I did promise you the world.'

'No other world I'd rather be,' I replied, holding his gaze. 'I love you. Always remember that.'

His eyebrows knitted together, like they often did when I said something vague or ominous. He pulled me close, wrapping me in the folds of his arms, kissing me in a crescent-shape from lips to neck.

That night, as he slept, I returned to the beach and watched the sky, waiting for the dark crescent to come. When it did, the shape was closer. I could make out the individual parts, a mosaic of spirits. Tomorrow, they'd be within reach.

~

I was ten when I first saw the dark crescent. Ma was gathering driftwood while I explored rockpools. She made wall hangings from broken pieces, with woven thread that would hang like seaweed from uneven frames. I liked that she was creative. That we had something in common.

I heard the sound first, the humming approach like a flutter of wings. 'What's that noise?'

Ma turned, eyes narrowed. 'Just the sea, sweetheart.'

The noise grew louder, closer, but Ma didn't seem to notice. That's when I saw it—the dark shadow of moving shapes across the water, looking down in a rictus grin. I stood up. 'What kind of birds are those?'

Ma stared at me. 'What birds?'

When I pointed, she followed my gaze, but said nothing. Could she not see them? To me, they were impossible to miss. She hurried me home after that, leaving the gathered treasure behind despite my protests.

Later, as she tucked me into bed, I asked her again about the shape in the sky.

'Nothing for you to worry about.'

'But what did they want?'

She stroked my hair. 'Did you know flying things can be messengers to other lands?'

I smiled and shook my head, settling in for one of her magical stories. She recounted tales of the otherworld—the land beneath the earth, the place where gods and spirits and dead things lived. I didn't understand death then, so it sounded like an exciting adventure.

She double-locked my window that night, bolted the shutters, sprinkled salt on the sill. She did that sometimes, usually on Samhain or before a storm. Finally, she hung a hand-woven dreamcatcher over my bed, then kissed me lightly on the cheek.

'I love you,' she said. 'Always remember that.'

The next morning, Ma was gone.

~

I understood now what Ma had done. And in turn, what I had to do next.

*No surer things than omens.*

No surer fate than death.

The waves were calm on the final night when I reached the shore. I took my shoes off, stepping into the water, feeling the soothing chill between my toes as the salt-tinged breeze kissed my cheeks.

Then, the humming began, and in the stillness, something rippled. A dark crescent matching the moon. It descended slow at first, then grew closer until I could see the spirits clearly. Forms billowed with blurred edges, limbs twisted and grotesque.

I stole a final look back at the cottage. The windows were shuttered, salt sprinkled over every entry. Nothing would get in. I'd left Alasdair a note explaining that I was leaving, that he shouldn't follow. He'd struggle with it at first, but it would save him the pain of thinking me gone without a trace. Hopefully he'd leave the island eventually. Move on, somewhere where darkness didn't dance, and omens kept their distance.

I turned back towards the dark crescent, the air changing around me. I stepped further into the water, ready, accepting my fate.

When the spirits took me, they carried me on the air, higher and higher, until I was part of the shroud. Then I was falling, descending fast as the humming turned to shrieks. But a single voice was clear amidst the cacophony. A familiar one.

'Nothing to worry about, sweetheart. Just the sea.'

# The Frittening

Sorley was on his way to bed when he heard the thump against his back window. He looked to the glass, expecting to see a crack in it, but there was no mark. He peered outside into the gloaming, looking for any sign of a bird on the ground below, but there was only a slight puddle underneath the window, even though it hadn't rained since the morning. Frowning, he saluted to the night, worried about birds in windows, dark skies, and omens. At least the bird wasn't in the cottage itself. Then he'd really be in trouble.

Still, he was uneasy when he headed up to his room and took extra care with his nightly routine. He checked under the bed, behind shutters, in wardrobes and dark corners. He made sure the horseshoe that hung above his bed was still secure, and that the line of salt along his windowsill wasn't broken. There was a jar of herbs that Myra had sold him, and tonight, for good measure, he sprinkled them around his bed. Then, content nothing could break in, he drew the curtains, blew the candles out and carefully slipped under his covers.

His sleep that night was disturbed by an intermittent thumping. Each time he heard the noise, he awoke slightly dazed, listened to the rhythmic *thump-thump*, before falling back to sleep. An uncomfortable knot began in his stomach, a dread that seeped into his thoughts, making him dream of strange shapes in dark corners of his room, reaching up and grabbing him by the legs, stealing him away to the otherworld. Sorley hadn't always taken the old tales seriously, but after what happened to Lou, he'd never ignored an omen.

The next morning, Sorley investigated everything around his home. Looked for leaks, or broken shutters, or damages to the wall. There was nothing that suggested any attempt at intrusion. No feathers to indicate a distressed bird, though the puddle underneath the back window was still there. He leaned down to touch it, and there was a strong thick smell coming from it. A stench that caught in his throat and made him gag. He boiled a kettle on the stove, then poured it over the puddle to wash it away. After three kettles-full the puddle was gone and, content, he headed out to his woodworking shed to get on with his daily work.

For three more mornings, the puddle appeared, and every night he heard the *thump-thump-thump* against his window. He washed the puddle away, and even began hanging wards up around his cottage, burnt some of Myra's sage to scare dark forces away. He used an entire bundle and kept the other in his pocket along with a woven dolly he'd bought from her last time at the market. Then, he sat on a bench outside, watching the haar roll in, until his hands grew too tense to sit in the cold salt sea air any longer. That night, when he heard the *thump* again, he ran to the window with his omen-wards in hand. The puddle was back with no apparent cause. Haunting him. So, he grabbed a scroll of paper and an inkwell from his desk, and hands shaking, began to write.

The next morning, after a sleepless night, he took his letter to Iver, one of his neighbouring farmers, and asked if he'd deliver the letter to Myra on his daily routes. He paid the farmer in coin he'd made from his latest fishing boat sale, more than was fair, given that it was on his way to one of his fields anyway. But Sorley wasn't one for confrontation, and he needed to see Myra, so he paid and returned home. He busied himself with woodworking in his shed outside, taking care over an oar he'd been making on commission for a wealthy family in town. In each, he inscribed a good luck symbol for seafaring, then shivered at the thought. Sorley would rarely head to the coast anymore, nor go near the water. Anything he built was sold on. There were too many dark and dangerous things in the sea, and there were already enough of them on the island to be worrying about as it was.

~

Myra received the note by wagon one morning, delivered by Iver, a stout farmer with arms as thick as his legs, strong from guiding his horse-drawn wagon around the island. He barely said a word to her as he dropped it off—he was one of the sceptics that, at worst, believed her to be a witch, and at best, a fraud. Still, he must have been paid to drop the letter off, and it was a small island—if she didn't get it, word would get around, and reputation on this island was as important as the tides. And as changeable as the weather.

Myra often received deliveries like this, outside of the courier days, from those who couldn't wait long to see her. It sometimes meant things were urgent, but more often than not it meant that her most loyal customer had been scared by a shadow again. As she turned the letter over, and saw her name written in scrawling ink in an untidy rushed hand, she knew it was the latter. *Sorley.* The man who lived in his cottage on the western peninsula, inland as far from the sea as he could get, who wrote to her every other week about some omen or other. Though, on her visits to him, she'd never found any sign of what he reported. Like the Kelpie he claimed to have seen coming out the sea one day, which turned out to be a cow that had escaped its field, or the washer woman by the river that was only some kids in town playing a prank with red paint and fake clothes to scare passersby. Then there was the case of the birds in the sky that was just a cloud formation, and though she agreed to wait with him in case the dreaded Sluagh came to claim him for the otherworld, lo and behold, days passed, and no spirit or demon came.

In an island full of omens, it wasn't uncommon for them to be misinterpreted. For her to be called upon to deal with phenomena that turned out to be only a natural change in weather or sea conditions, or just the screech of an owl, rather than a banshee or siren song. Around a quarter of all her requests included actual threats or foretellings of doom. But Sorley's requests had grown more and more frantic over the years. Sometimes he would even call upon her because he'd simply walked under a ladder, accidentally killed a spider, or had dropped a knife inside his cottage. Even though she knew such small things wouldn't lead to anything dangerous, she would still bring wards just to put his mind at ease.

So, Myra didn't open the letter straight away, and instead busied herself with her herbs, drying and separating lavender, bog myrtle, and sage, tying them in bundles or wee bottles with stoppers when done. The herbs had some effect, but mostly she sold them for omen protection after removing the threat, because the islanders liked something physical to reassure them. After, she made her usual daily trinkets—charms to charge later in the moonlight, and little woven dollies to ward off evil. Those brought in more coin than anything—people liked to pre-empt omens before they showed themselves.

Supplies restocked, she piled them in a basket ready for the market the following day. The job of an omen-hunter was a varied one, but it paid her way and kept her busied and useful. It also meant people didn't often seek out her company in case somehow the omens she encountered rubbed off on her, and then on them. But truth be told she enjoyed the quiet life on her little corner of the island.

Her morning chores done, she sat down with a cup of steaming camomile tea. She opened the letter from Sorley, reading it with narrowed eyes and a frown that grew deeper as she got further down. The handwriting became more and more erratic with every sentence. After, she placed the letter down and sighed. A *puddle*—probably a drainage issue, which would explain the rotten smell. The thump against the window could be anything—the wind creaking between loose panes, a rat or mouse in the walls, or simply the rain, which would also explain the puddle. Still, even though Sorley had an overactive sense of omens, she never refused the call of a customer, and she'd grown quite protective of Sorley over the years, especially after what happened with his wife. So, she packed up a small cart of supplies, tethered up her goat, Gwyn, to the front, and began on her way to the western part of the island.

~

Since sending the letter, Sorley had sat nervously worrying at the pendant charm around his neck while looking out to sea and avoiding focussing too much on anything in case an omen flashed across the sky or in the wind, or in case he spotted a creature lurking on the dark sea horizon. Close to the cliffside shore, which was visible on a clear day like today, he spotted a rowboat—one of his own—with one of his neighbours and his daughter aboard, fishing. He clung his pendant tighter and looked instead at his feet, tutting about irresponsible parents and bemoaning how he'd come to live on such an island. Finally, as the grey sky turned blue, and the afternoon sun rose pale into the sky, he heard the trundle of Myra's cart approach.

He stood, headed to the front of the cottage. There, he greeted her with a smile and gave Gwyn the goat a pat between her horns. Gwyn bleated and nibbled on his woollen jumper, pulling at the loose threads. Myra gave him the same look she always did—the kind that told him she thought he was just being paranoid again. But at least she'd come, and he ushered her inside.

'Maybe I can see the puddle first?' she mused.

'Oh, yes, of course, yes, follow me.' He led her to the spot underneath the back window, where the puddle had gathered, still giving off its awful stench.

Myra scrunched up her face as she leant down to examine it. Braver than he was, she touched the ground around it softly, tracking the edges of the puddle. 'The ground is very wet here,' she observed.

'I've been washing it away with boiling water.'

'And your drainage, where does that usually come out?'

'Just along here to the side of the cottage, but I already checked and there are no blockages to the pipes.'

'Hmm.' Myra glanced between his woodworking shed and the cottage. 'You use varnish for your boats?'

Sorley nodded. 'Aye, of course, why does that matter?'

'I'm not questioning your work, just wondered if there is a vat through there might be leaking.' She gestured towards the shed. 'Could explain it.'

He shook his head firm. 'I'm sure that's not it. Besides, what about the smell?'

She shrugged. 'Some chemical reactions create strange odours. I see it in my tonics all the time.'

'Well, say it is that, how do you explain the thumping?'

Myra smiled. 'Why don't you show me where you hear it?'

Begrudging her doubting him, Sorley headed inside and pointed at the window and the walls. 'I hear it loudest down here, like it's hitting against the building or glass.'

'Like what's hitting it? How loud, how strong?'

'Well,' Sorley took his time to answer carefully. 'I thought at first it might be a bird, but it was slightly softer than that. Like it was muffled a wee bit. You know, like an echo.'

'A shutter?'

'Checked them.'

'Maybe a drip in the walls, which could explain the leak.'

'No, there's no leak,' he insisted getting agitated now. 'There's something trying to get into my cottage!'

'Something you can't see?'

He nodded his head once. 'That's right, but don't most omens only reveal themselves in time?'

'You think this might be an omen, then?'

'Yes. I do.'

Her voice softened. 'Now Sorley, I know you take omens very seriously, as do I, but what do I always say to you?'

He sighed. 'That there are many false omens, and we only need to look close enough to see them wrong.'

'Indeed,' she smiled.

'But this one is *real*, Myra, I know it. I have this… I don't know, sinking feeling, in the pit of my stomach, like this *thing* that's causing the puddles is watching me, waiting to take me away to the otherworld.'

Myra sighed. 'Why don't we sit and have some tea inside? I have a special herbal blend in the cart.'

The kitchen soon filled with the scent of nettles and winterberries as Myra brewed her concoction on the stove, leaving Sorley rocking back and forth on his chair.

'Now,' Myra said. 'I understand unknown things are scary, and I know after what happened to Lou that you're more cautious than most. But it might be time we try to wean you off your wards and omen-chasing. Maybe it will help you find some peace.'

Sorley felt his stomach tighten and he shook his head, chasing the memory of his wife away. The day before she'd left him, a bird had flown into their home, and Lou had caught it before gently releasing it outside. The next morning she walked straight out into the sea and never came back. 'This isn't about Lou.'

'That thump, you said you thought it was a bird at first. Is that why it made you jumpy? Because of-'

Sorley stood up and clenched the table. 'This isn't about her. And you shouldn't speak about it like that. Not here.'

Myra's face was impassive. 'I'm sorry, Sorley. I didn't mean to upset you.'

'Are you going to help me or not? With a ward, or token, or some tonic you might have?'

'If that's what you need, I can certainly give you something.'

'Then I'll take what you've got. There's plenty coin if that's what you're worried about.'

Myra bristled. 'I'm not.' she took a long, drawn-out sip on her teacup then stood up calmly and slowly. 'I'll get some supplies from the cart.'

~

Myra left Sorley's cottage feeling uneasy. Not because of any omen, but she probably shouldn't have brought up his wife. She thought maybe it would be helpful, push him to confront his past, to see he didn't need to be afraid of every gust of wind. He'd barely spoken a word to her as she'd readied her wards. She cleansed the puddle first with sage smoke, sprinkled special salt around the area, then sat whispering a quiet incantation by the spot, though she only spoke a jumble of words. There was no omen to frighten off as far as she was concerned, so she just made it look convincing. After, Sorley gave her a sharp nod and shoved some coin into her hands, though she took only enough to cover the herbs and gave the rest back.

Back home, she settled in by the fire and thought as she often did of the omens, and the ones that were sometimes dangerous and real. It was why she'd become what she was, but often she found herself wondering if the omens themselves were really as strong as was said. No doubt they had power, but sometimes the omens were made worse by the islanders' reactions to them. No one had ever been able to explain what possessed Lou to step outside that morning, into the waves, to never come home.

~

The puddle didn't return by the back window the next day. It appeared instead by the front door, and when Sorley almost stepped on it in the morning after his first restful sleep in weeks, he cried out so loud that he startled a bird nearby. It cawed and flew straight at him. He ducked and dodged it, shielded his eyes as the flutter of wings thrashed around him, but when he looked up again it was gone, flying away from the house towards the sea.

Gathering what was left of his wits, he knelt down by the new puddle. It had the same awful smell. He did his usual warding off with sage and salt, considered writing to Myra again but wondered if she'd even come after what she'd said yesterday. He wasn't even sure he wanted her here after that.

That night, he decided he would stay up to find proof of the puddle's source. So, he set up a chair staring at the front door, with a mallet of his own making in hand. If a demon or spirit crept out of the darkness, he'd be ready for it.

Sorley stayed awake for as long as he could keep his eyes open. He hummed to himself, busied his mind with trying to name the types of trees on the island. But by the time he reached pine, his mind drifted and a troubled sleep took him.

He dreamt of Lou, of her voice calling out to him. She was in the sea, only her ankles covered by the water, and she was luminescent in the moonlight with dark black hair dripping and dripping in a *thump-thump* noise into the darkness below. Then the waves against the rocks, *thump-thump*. The pebbles crackling together as he walked towards Lou, *thump-thump*. His heartbeat as he grew closer and closer, *thump-thump*. And when he reached out his hand to grab her, he found himself falling into the waves.

He woke up with his head lying flat against the front wall, his cheek numb from the cold and stone. And there it was again, the puddle. He sat up sharply. His mallet was gone. Then he noticed something was different. The puddle was trickling slowly down a pathway. A trail towards the sea.

~

Myra hadn't heard from Sorley for days when she began to grow worried. There was no letter with the courier, no sign of him at the market where he usually came to sell his wooden wares and buy her wards. When she asked around town about him, Iver eventually told her he'd seen Sorley walking towards the beach. Myra felt a deep unease, and she closed up her market stall early and headed towards the western shore. She stopped by Sorley's cottage first and knocked on the door, but no one was in. At the back, she checked his woodworking shed and found only an unfinished boat sitting upturned on its brackets. At the back window, the puddle was gone, and her salts were still spread around the walls.

Leaving Gwyn and her cart by the shed, she ran down towards the westward beach. There she saw a figure hunched over in the sand. He held a mallet and was rocking back and forth staring at the flotsam and jetsam around him. The pungent smell of seaweed filled the air, and she wrinkled her nose at the other scent that mingled. Something putrid, stronger, like dead rotten fish. Hesitantly she reached out for Sorley. He was freezing cold and soaking wet.

'Sorley, are you okay?'

He didn't even look up at her. He just kept staring at the beach. He appeared to have used the mallet to dig a hole in the sand, and at the base of the hole was a small puddle of water.

'You see it now?' Sorley said in a hushed whisper. 'Down there.'

'Sorley,' she began gently. 'Puddles like that form in sand when you dig deep enough.'

'No, not the puddle. Don't you see it. It's right there. The frittening.'

Myra had never heard the word before. 'What are you talking about?'

But Sorley didn't answer, and when Myra tried to get him to stand

and come home, he let out a wailing sound and refused to budge. So, Myra took some blankets and tea down, wrapped him up warm as best she could and poured out some tea which he sipped slowly. But he wouldn't stop staring at the puddle in the sand.

~

A couple of days passed, and Myra ran out of suggestions of what to do with him. She'd created a makeshift shelter around him and brought him food which he would eat slowly. But he never left the spot and never stopped staring at the hole. She paid Iver to come down to try and help her move him, but as soon as anyone touched him, Sorley screamed out a wail that set dread in their stomachs.

'Curse you,' he said. 'Curse all of you.'

The farmer shrugged and gave up, much to Myra's annoyance, and as a slight old woman herself there was no way she could force Sorley away from the beach. She even tried casting wards around him to chase off any omen that might have settled nearby, but if there was an omen it had already taken root, though she couldn't see what he claimed to see on the beach. He would mutter 'frittening', 'boneless', 'spineless' over and over, and occasionally in hushed whispers she heard him say his wife's name too.

Myra visited him every day to check he was still there, still alive, and every day he remained. Then, one morning she arrived and found him surrounded by an entire flock of sheep. And it was the strangest thing. They were all standing in a perfect circle with Sorley at the centre, staring at the hole Sorley had dug. The eeriest part was that the sheep were entirely silent. Not a single bleat amongst them.

It didn't take long for Iver to show up looking for his missing herd. He tried to move them, tugged at them one by one, but the sheep, although breaking out of the trance that Sorley was in, wouldn't leave with him. They simply roamed the beach aimlessly.

When word got around, the islanders, of course, grew fearful. Fearful of whatever curse had fallen upon them, and they blamed Sorley for it all. There was a community meeting, and it was agreed that Sorley had to be dealt with. Before they could come up with anything more nefarious, Myra offered to try something else.

She started by creating a sleeping tonic to put in Sorley's tea. She didn't like using them if she had any other choice—they could cause confusion, distress, especially for already fragile minds. As many of the islanders watched on from behind the beach one evening, Myra brought

Sorley some tea. He drank it slowly and eventually fell sideways into a slumber. Iver helped Myra put Sorley into his wagon and they brought him back up to his bed to sleep it off. Myra then returned to the beach where the sheep were now sitting in a circle, asleep near the hole. Myra covered it up, cast some wards, spoke some protection spells, then for good measure, poured some herbs and tonics over it. Still unsure what she was dealing with, she hoped it would be enough. She returned to Sorley's cottage and set up a makeshift bed in the living space.

Myra was awoken by a *thump-thump* on Sorley's door. She sat up and unlocked the front door to find a red-faced Iver. His clothes were red too, covered in blood. He immediately made to step inside, but Myra held her hand on the frame.

'He up there?' Iver demanded.

'Why, what's happened?'

'My sheep,' he said. 'He's done something. Cursed 'em.'

Myra looked again at the blood on his hands. 'What happened?'

'Found em on the beach all bloody and messed up. Rotten with such a stench.' His voice was a mix of anger, fear, desperation. 'Every single one.' He paused and took a breath, gestured towards the beach. 'Don't know why, but they were up on that cliff edge by the beach. Found some of their wool there at the top, and then they must've jumped right off. Straight down into the rocks. What'd drive em to that, eh?'

'I don't know,' Myra said, fighting the instinct to look behind her and upstairs, to implicate Sorley and the puddle, and whatever else was going on. 'But Sorley's been here all night. Door's been locked; I've been downstairs.'

'It's his fault, I know it. He was staring down there in the sand, and then all of a sudden, my sheep…did he lead them there? Is that how he got them on the beach in the first place?'

'I'm so sorry,' Myra said. 'I'll go there now, investigate, see if I can-'

'Don't want any of your wards or false tricks. This is as much your fault as his. You should've dealt with Sorley months ago.'

'Dealt with?'

'Aye, after Lou. You've been playing along with his fantasies, his delusions. Pretending like your omen-hunting is real when I know it's all a load of old wives' tales.'

Myra resisted the urge to defend herself as the farmer continued.

'And now he's gone and done this to my sheep. What'd they ever do to him? I've been bringing some of those up since they were wee lambs. Their wool is what keeps folks on the island warm at night.' He gestured to Myra's own jumper. 'See, even you. Even *him*.' He stepped back and pointed to the upstairs window.

'I'm sure that whatever happened to your sheep, it wasn't him.' But she was lying. She didn't know for sure he wasn't involved. She'd not checked the back door. If it was unlocked, could he have gotten out there, tempted the sheep from the beach, led them up to the cliff? But why would he?

'Well, you better sort him out. And if he comes near any more of my animals, I'll make him answer for it myself,' he said, and he spun back around and headed down the path. He paused at seeing Myra's cart, and Gwyn grazing outside. 'You better keep an eye on that goat of yours too.'

Myra wasn't sure whether it was a threat, so she made sure to keep Gwyn close, tying her up behind the house near the shed for the time being. Then she headed upstairs. Sorley was still fast asleep, and she was relieved until she spotted his muddy boots at the base of his bed, small tufts of grass imprinted into the base of them. She bent down to touch them. Still wet. Downstairs, she found the back door unlocked.

She headed to the cliff herself. On the rocks below, blood stained the highest jagged rocks that couldn't be washed clean by the sea. Iver had piled the sheep on the shore, the sand streaked red with blood. In all her time working on this island, she'd never come across an omen as violent. A sign of illness or death or two, but never with such intentional malice. That sort of malice she'd only ever seen between other people.

She headed back up to Sorley's cottage unsure what she should do. He slept all day with a fever, and seemed like he would sleep all night, so she locked the doors up again and allowed herself to rest her eyes.

~

Myra was woken once again by a thump, but this time it was louder and came with a whistle of wind. The back door was hanging open. She tiptoed outside. Gwyn was gone too. There were little hoof marks in the mud, alongside bare footprints. Sorley.

Rushing now, panic rising in her like a building wave, she ran towards the beach. In the moonlight, she spotted a figure on the cliff, looking over the edge. In Sorley's hands was Gwyn, held out to the sky and bleating bloody murder. Myra ran as fast as she could, out of the cottage and down the winding path towards the cliff. Just in time, she managed to pull Sorley back. Gwyn escaped his grasp, avoided falling over the edge, and ran inland, into the long dune grasses.

'What are you doing?' Myra said to him. 'Is this what you did to the sheep?'

'Was the frittening made me do it. Look,' he said, and he held his hands out. They were slightly damp, but his hands were empty.

'There's nothing in your hands, Sorley. Let's get you home so we can talk…'

'No. You'll see.' His voice was suddenly deep. 'The sea calls now. She calls. Lou's there too. But don't worry about me, you'll understand soon enough.' Sorley raised his hands to his chest and smiled.

Before Myra could stop him, Sorley jumped away from the cliff towards the sea. There was no sound of impact, rocks, sea, or otherwise. When she ran down to the beach to look for him, there wasn't any sign of him in the waves. To her left, the stench of the sheep cloyed at her throat, and she was sick in the dune grass. She watched the water, helpless, until the sun came up and she knew Sorley was really gone.

He and Lou were together now. The thought brought no comfort.

Dawn broke, and Gwyn came down from the hill, nudged Myra's hand to tempt her back up and away from the beach. With a final look at Sorley's cottage, and the puddle that no longer existed, she packed her cart back up and headed home.

~

The envelope arrived from a courier some weeks later, a request from another islander. As Myra read the words within a chill spread across her body. The letter mentioned a persistent puddle, a lingering stench, and a *thump-thump-thump* at the window.

# Nesting



*Her jaw aches, like claws are pulling at her teeth, as if searching for parts, removing them one by one until there's nothing left but a gaping maw, and there are stones in her throat so that she can't breathe, then something tickles her cheek like a feather or a fine paint brush, and everything is dark, immobilised, like she's no longer in control of her own body, time to wake up, time to wake up, but it's not working and she wants to scream but all that comes out is a retch that echoes into the never ending darkness.*

The nest appeared on the first morning of my retreat. I didn't notice it initially, nestled in a nook in the corner as if hiding a tiny mouse hole. It was made, as nests usually are, with broken twigs, brittle and dry, woven into a labyrinthine basin. No eggs were inside, nor feathers or hint of usual habitation. Instead, there were tiny pebbles, white and smooth and shiny. I picked them up one by one and counted them. Thirty-two in total.

*Odd.*

I checked the window to make sure there were no gaps. Like many old buildings, the panes were at an angle, so that the wood creaked, and the hinges rattled. But the only spaces between were tiny air pockets that were just big enough to let a spider through.

The sun was still low in the sky and the clouds were painted a rusty orange. The view from the window was even more idyllic than it had been the night before—a craggy cliff overlooking an endless ocean, exactly the kind of escape I'd wanted to finish the last piece of my collection.

I looked down at the nest again. It's an old house, I thought. It must have been there the night before, and I hadn't noticed because it was dark when I'd arrived. I scooped it up carefully, cradled it in my hands and felt the surface of the pebbles again. A stabbing pain shot to my jaw, and I clenched it. I really needed to go to the dentist about that wisdom tooth when I got home.

I took the nest outside and left it on the picnic bench, then set myself up in the living room. Placing a sheet on the floor, I angled my easel in the middle, facing the window so that I could see the trees behind the cottage move back and forth in their secret whisper outside. No one would disturb me here. I propped the blank canvas up and tried to summon a creative image in my mind. Shapes began to form, so I picked up the palette—selecting black, white, blue, and emerald green—and started painting wherever the brush took me.

By the end of the day, I'd barely finished the background, but the outline of something was starting to take form—splashes of colours danced amidst blurry edges.

Later, as I made dinner, I glanced out to the garden and saw the nest sitting there in the soft light of the moon. Something about it was making me curious, like an itch I needed to scratch. So, I took it back inside and washed the pebbles in the sink until they were shiny and polished. Back at my easel, I stared at the dashes of colour in front of me. I knew there had been something missing—the pebbles were the perfect addition, so I stuck them on carefully with glue and paint. A beak had formed.

~

*She's surrounded by bright light and she can't make a sound for it's as though her mouth has been sewn shut, and it's still and quiet here, lying on her back facing the light, then in the brightness a flash of black and white plumage breaks through and she can just make out a bird—a magpie—soaring towards her, and it lands, starts to dance on her abdomen, searching, as if trying to find a worm, though it's alone, solitary, so she tries to salute it, but her arms are stuck, the sorrow will come, and now it's jumping on her stomach, the talons digging into flesh, she screams, it hurts so much, digging and digging, and then from its beak she sees what looks like a worm, covered in red and white, and the magpie looks at her with a tilted head, a blink of its green-grey eyes, and it jumps away, flying into brightness.*

~

It appeared again the next morning. This time it lay on the windowsill as I looked out into the bright breaking haar across the sea. I couldn't be sure if it was the same nest, but it was in the same intricate shape. I peered inside expecting pebbles again, but instead a piece of rope, curved and twisted, was curled up in the centre. It was covered in red dirt and stringy fibres like it had only recently been dug up from the earth. What sort of creature collects pieces of rope? I opened the window and lifted it inside.

The rope was rough in my hands, fibres bristling against my skin. It felt oddly familiar, as if it were a missing piece to some puzzle I didn't understand. My stomach twisted like a flutter of wings and grumbled angrily at me. I took the rope with me as I went downstairs, soaking it in the sink so that the water turned red. After I'd finished my breakfast, the rope had bulged out in size, so I left it to dry on the aga while I worked.

As the day wore on, the painting wove with colour. My hand seemed to move of its own free will, colour cresting and twisting like crashing waves. Slowly a body started to appear, then a beady eye, and an ivory stomach. But I just couldn't get the feet right.

I sat back and stared at the painting until it grew dark outside. I looked at the pebbles that formed the beak and had an idea. The rope was dry, so I started to pluck at the threads, pulling bits off and positioning them beneath the stomach, until talons appeared, sharp and deadly. In the dim light of the room, they looked almost like they were moving, as if they could reach from the canvas at any moment. Satisfied, I covered the paint palette in film. I'd leave the wings for the next morning.

~

*She's lying on her front while a creature pecks at her back, but she can't see what it's doing, it just pulls and digs, a euphoric pain ebbs into her body, and the skin and muscle peels away until bone is reached, and she feels the tug then, like she's being ripped apart and suddenly the pain is too much, but she can't move her arms to bat the bird away, it simply digs relentlessly until it extracts the piece it needs, and she feels a deep ache in her lungs as if the cage protecting them has been broken, and the darkness comes swift and unyielding.*

~

On the third morning, I found the window open, even though I was sure I had shut it the night before. I shivered, feeling my way around the room, searching for any hint of intrusion. But there was, of course, none. Maybe the next retreat should be somewhere less remote, though I did enjoy the freedom this place gave me—it allowed me to be absorbed by my painting, to really give myself to the art. The end result was always better that way.

It was a bright day for the start of autumn, and light spilled in through the sash windows of the kitchen when I ventured downstairs. But something caught my eye as I was filling the kettle. Sitting on the armchair, resting on the soft cushion was a nest. It was a little bigger than before, to accommodate the item within. A piece of driftwood, white and hollow and curved, lay safely within its walls.

As I leant down to inspect it closer, a pain shot into my ribs, and I had to steady myself on the armrest. The moment passed quickly—I blamed the mattress for being too soft. I picked up the driftwood carefully. It was light and felt smooth like porcelain. I set it down on the table and realised its shape was odd, thin at one end and thick at the bottom with little ridges jutting out—almost like a broken wing without its feathers.

My mind wandered to my incomplete painting, knowing this was the perfect part. Ignoring the now-whistling kettle, I took the driftwood and presented it to my canvas. It slotted in perfectly beneath the curved black plumage, the flash of emerald green tail, the rope feet and the pebbled beak. After I had glued it on, I drew the final line, connecting the beak to the tail.

And I felt a deep ache in my muscles. My head spun as the room moved. I tried to steady my breathing, but it was no use—I was already falling.

*The world is blurry again as she feels like her body is being pulled apart, piece by piece, limb by limb and reconstructed into a strange whole, and she can't breathe as the morphing continues, all she wants is for it to stop, she can't open her eyes and there's just a constant stabbing pain of stretching and pulling and compressing and she's shrinking, her body itches with strange barbs bristling out of her, until all she can do is curl into a ball and let the night take her.*

I'm awake, though something feels off. Moonlight drifts through the panes and there's a whistle of air in the room. But the space is too big for me, and everything looks out of perspective. I blink and look up at the bed. A figure is lying there, sleeping. My mind is foggy, like I'm still in a dream.

I glance at my feet and clawed talons stretch out. Underneath them is a nest that looks oddly familiar, broken twigs knotted together into a labyrinthine structure. But it's empty, and a nest shouldn't be empty.

I'm drawn towards the sleeping figure, a woman with gleaming hair. There's a paint set by her bed, clean, shiny, and untouched. A clock ticks slowly, second by second. Then it stills and all I can hear is the sound of her breathing. Her mouth is open, a gaping maw with walls of glittering moonlit silver—thirty-two pebbles in a row. Just the parts I need. I lean in and pluck the pebbles out, one by one, placing them carefully in the nest. After, I gaze upon the creation, feeling a warmth in my beak.

I push the nest into the corner by the window and hop up to the sill. A chill wind ruffles my feathers. But it will be sunrise soon. I'll come back tomorrow, and the next day, to work on my creations, nesting, until my collection is done.

# Wisp in the Dark

The gate to the cemetery at the end of my road was locked after dark, but I knew the way in. Hidden behind overgrown bramble bushes was a crumbling gap in the wall, just small enough to crawl through. I collected some brambles on the way in, ate a few and pocketed the rest. The bitterness of them matched the cold tang in the air. I wiped the juice on my coat, streaks of dark red stark against my waterproof grey.

I didn't need a torch here, because the light was already waiting. It hovered a few feet away, a ball of silvery white under the root-rotted branches of a skeletal tree.

*Meet me under the dead elm tree, where the earth is ash and the spirits run free.*

In the soft light of the ghostly wisp, the tree appeared to be dancing. Branches like gnarled limbs moved from side to side, willing me forwards. Willing me to follow the wisp. I skipped towards it, but it danced away, dipping between the shrubbery, along an overgrown path, leading me in twists and turns until we reached the steps in the centre. There, it settled, bobbing like a floating lantern. Above, a magpie, disturbed by my arrival, cawed then took flight with a flutter of wings. I said hello and saluted it, like Mum always taught me, to chase the bad omen away.

I turned to the wisp, which was waiting patiently. It seemed calm today, its light softer than usual. Cautiously, I approached it. 'Hi,' I said, reaching into my pockets and holding out the brambles, half squashed in my pocket. 'I brought you a gift.' The wisp drifted over, its shape stretching and morphing. Then a transparent hand reached out. I watched, eyes wide, as it tickled my palm. An ice-coldness grasped my arm, and the wisp flashed dark red, matching the streak on my coat. My breath caught, but I kept my hand deathly still.

*Bring me gifts, a trinket or treasure, help make me whole, and I'll give you forever.*

Afterwards, the ghostly hand retracted, and the brambles had turned to ash. I let the dust sprinkle to the ground like sand from an hourglass.

'I brought sandwiches too.' I sat on the step and split the bread in half, a triangle for me, a triangle for the wisp. 'Peanut butter, hope that's okay.'

The wisp floated over to me again, and it moved across the sandwich. After a moment, the bread turned to dust just like the brambles, but this time the wisp flashed orange and expanded a little. There was even a flicker, almost like a smile. We had milk and cookies for dessert.

The wisp didn't speak, because it didn't have a mouth—not yet at least, but then it didn't have a hand three days ago either—yet something about it made me feel at ease, like I could tell it everything. I'd speak stories and secrets into the quiet night and the wisp would listen. I didn't have many friends at school. Mostly people ignored me, like I was invisible. Soon, I'd probably just be the weird kid that hung around the cursed cemetery, appeasing and befriending spirits, or whatever this wisp was. But I liked it here. With the wisp, that I think, liked me too.

'Mum's making apple pie tomorrow,' I told the wisp as I was leaving. 'I'll bring you a piece.'

There was a gust in the air, and I swear on the wind I heard a single word, quiet and lilting. *Delicious.*

~

Every night, I snuck out the house, each time bringing offerings more and more extravagant. Biscuits, cheese, birthday cake, marshmallows, chocolate-dipped strawberries. Mum found my stash of food one afternoon, hidden under my bed in preparation for the night ahead.

'It's for my friend that lives down the road,' I told her, in a half lie, when she asked me about it.

Her eyebrows arched. 'We're the last house on this road?'

'Well,' I began carefully. 'My friend is there, and gets hungry. I just want to help.'

Understanding stretched across her face. 'Oh. Do you think I might get to meet this friend?'

I shook my head. 'They don't like to be around other people.'

'No, of course they don't,' she said, her smile vague, and I wondered if she knew about the wisp. But how could she? I was the only one that visited the wisp. It was my secret. 'Does this friend go to your school?'

I bit down on my lip. 'No. It's too crowded there.'

'You know you can tell me if anything is wrong, at school? I know kids can be cruel, and if you need a friend to speak to, I'm here.' She squeezed my shoulders, kissed me lightly on the forehead, and I realised that she didn't think my friend from down the road was real. That I'd made it up. Maybe it was better for her to think that, and when the time came, when it had grown enough, I could introduce her to the wisp. But not yet. Telling her now would mean telling her that I snuck out at night, and I'd be grounded for weeks if she found out.

'I'm fine, Mum,' I said. 'Everything's fine.'

~

Over the weeks, with my nightly offerings, the wisp grew and grew. Limbs became more permanent, solid, and soon it had morphed into a human-like shape.

*When my hunger grows, my form will wither, but as I grow full, I'll go hither and thither.*

'Do you like it here?' I asked as we wandered between gravestones, the wisp walking on almost-legs.

No reply, but another breeze tickled my cheek, tinged with the scent of gorse and fresh earth. The wisp still had no mouth, just a formless head, and indents where I imagined eyes might be.

'I think it's peaceful,' I said. 'Not like school, and other places. Do you have a name?' As I walked, I read engraved names out loud, imagining one of them could be my wisp friend. Magda, or Fred, or Gwyneth, or Juniper—June for short. I liked that. The wisp seemed like it could be a June.

'Can I call you June?'

No reply, but the wisp stretched out a long hand. Cold fingers intertwined with mine. Almost like the real thing.

'June,' I repeated, squeezing the hand lightly. 'See you tomorrow.'

As I headed home, a whisper whistled through the air. *June. Tomorrow. Hungry.'*

~

The next night, I returned with a picnic basket filled with treats, a flask of hot chocolate and a tartan blanket to sit on. It was Mum's suggestion, said that maybe if I put it together, she could come and join us on an afternoon adventure to meet June—by then I'd told her the wisp's name, because she wouldn't stop asking questions about my friend. But I didn't want Mum to join us yet, so I made it up on my own so I could bring it with me to the cemetery, where June and I could enjoy it instead.

The cemetery was bathed in moonlight when I crawled through the wall-gap. But something was off. No wisp of light greeted me by the dead elm tree. Instead, a girl stood under it, hair stretching to her waist, wearing a white dress too light for the season, silvery eyes aglow. Dark red smudges wrapped around her lips and fingertips—the last of the year's brambles. The girl had no shoes, and her feet were pockmarked with dirt, though she didn't show any sign of being cold. My stomach twisted. I didn't like seeing anyone else in the cemetery at night. No one else was supposed to know my secret. And maybe she'd scared June away.

'Why are you here? What did you do to June?'

She looked at me, tilted her head, and smiled. 'Don't you recognise me?'

The words sent a chill travelling down my spine, her voice familiar. 'You're…June?'

She laughed, and her voice pierced the silent night with a shrill force. If it was June, then she was different. 'Thank you for your offerings,' she said. 'But I'm still hungry. And I've been here for far too long.'

I stepped back, but it was too late. June was running towards me, hands held out like claws. And then she was singing and chanting, her words strange. Disjointed.

*'And here I'll roam, until comes another, to take my place, and I'll take the other.'*

Darkness enveloped me. For a long time, I couldn't see or speak or move. When the darkness finally dissolved, I was cloaked instead in an ethereal light. I was in the cemetery, and a girl was standing before me— no, not a girl, it was me. Dressed in waterproof grey, a red stain on her coat. She—I—was staring up at me, head tilted.

*'What's going on?'* I asked, but my words sounded distant and vague.

'I'm sorry. This was the only way,' the girl said, in *my* voice.

*'June?'*

'Thank you for taking my place,' she said. 'In exchange I've given you forever.' With a rictus grin, she picked up the picnic basket, broke a biscuit in half and left it on the roots of the dead elm tree. 'To keep you going, until you find another.' Then, she took a final look at me, and basket in hand, snuck off towards the bramble bush, disappearing into the night.

I tried to follow, but every time I approached the walls, I found myself back at the tree, feeling stretched and tired. And so very hungry. I turned and looked back at the biscuit. I tried to reach out a hand, but I no longer had one. Instead, I floated over it. It was bitter and stale, but it was something. My body stretched and the biscuit turned to ash.

As I roamed the cemetery, my memories drifted away like wisps in the wind.

I float between the tombstones, day and night, waiting and watching for visitors, but they never see me. Never hear me. Sometimes I follow them, call out, but no one listens, or they choose not to hear.

The other day, a girl came with her mum for a picnic, sitting together on a tartan blanket. I floated by the steps and watched them, smiling, laughing, feeling like they were something from a dream. At one point, the girl stopped and looked straight at me, as if she could see me. But then a magpie fluttered behind and flew into the trees above.

'Don't forget to say hello to Mr Magpie, and give him a salute,' the woman said. 'To chase the omens away.'

The girl smiled and saluted to the place where the bird had been. 'Hello,' she said. 'We've met before.'

Together they ate peanut butter sandwiches and apple pie. That night, I swept up the crumbs they'd left behind.

This afternoon I saw a boy. Young, quiet, hair dark as the earth. He was walking his dog under the old elm tree, and when it stopped to sniff the dark roots, he sat down at the base.

*Meet me under the dead elm tree, where the earth is ash and the spirits run free.*

He took an apple from his pocket, chewed at the edges, and dropped most of it with the core on the ground. I drifted over to him, reached a ghostly hand out over the leftover core and turned it to dust. He stared at me wide-eyed. He could see me. Finally, a friend.

*'Bring me gifts, a trinket or treasure, help make me whole, and I'll give you forever,'* I whispered, my voice carrying on the wind.

He smiled and his eyes filled with wonder, and I knew he'd return.

So, now I'm waiting under the dead elm tree, the ash, the earth, the spirits, and me.

And it's the perfect night for a picnic.

# The Taxidermist

The murdered crow sits mounted on a rowan tree in the centre of the market square. Immaculate, except for its eyes, which have been removed, too cleanly to have been pecked out by carrion.

Reyn leans over my shoulder. 'The Taxidermist. It has to be.'

I nod, slow. 'Where's this familiar's witch?'

'In mourning, like the rest.'

'Not you.'

'No.' She looks down as though expecting her own familiar to be looping around her ankles. 'Not me.' Her fox was one of The Taxidermist's early victims. Reyn still dresses in funerary-black, satin gloves covering her arms, a scarf around her neck.

I leave the bird and step over the cordon left by the Order—it's only there for show, anyway. They stopped investigating weeks ago. Dozens of familiars dead or missing in the Outers is enough to attract their attention, but not enough to warrant action. Until events reach College or Parliament, they won't waste their time. Reyn's the only one left with energy to keep looking. And now me. Because of Reyn's deep pockets, and refusal to take no for an answer.

'Do you feel its soul?' Reyn asks as we leave.

I stop in my tracks. 'What do you mean?'

'Can't you communicate with the dead? Because your kind are half in and out of the Otherworld.'

'My kind?'

She lowers her voice. 'The cat thing. Sorry, I didn't mean to offend.'

'Who told you?' The question comes out in a hiss, annoyingly not disproving her theory.

'I...no one,' she says. 'I'm observant—that's all—and see this city better than most.'

'You've been following me?'

'No.' She glances to the crow again, flaps her arms like a bird with broken wings. 'I just…wanted someone to help me.' She stares at her feet again, hands tensing as if calling her fox's ghost up for protection.

I soften.

'So, you know what I am, and still asked for help. Why?'

'Well…' She looks up, unblinking. 'I have an idea.'

~

Back at my office, Reyn tells me her plan, then sits patiently awaiting my response. It's not the worst idea: pretend to be Reyn's familiar in cat form, bait the killer, shift again, catch them in the act. But there are so many variables, and this isn't exactly my usual gig. I deal with stolen objects, marital affairs, occasional bounties for the Order. Nothing like this.

'It's too dangerous,' I say.

'We'd be careful. We just need to do something to catch The Taxidermist's attention,' Reyn says, an edge to her voice. 'Please. I have to avenge her.'

'I'm not sure I can.'

'Look.' Her voice sharpens. 'If we—you—solve this, everyone will come to you with their problems. And coin.'

I hesitate. She's right. If I caught The Taxidermist, there'd be no end to work. And, truthfully, this case bothered me even before Reyn approached me. Every week, the murders becoming more staged. And each time the killer takes the eyes —why the eyes? It's hard to ignore the macabre curiosity of that alone. 'Maybe…'

Her eyes brighten, and she hands me a full-to-bursting purse. 'Half now, half after?'

'I need to do some research first.'

'Of course.' She brings out a paper scroll. 'My address. Meet me there tomorrow, just after dark.'

As she leaves, I open the purse. She's lined the base with catnip. A nice touch.

~

That night, I head towards The Archives, a grand and grey Order building, with an ornate façade. If familiars went missing near here, there'd be no end to investigations. Curfews, searches, generous bounties.

Inside, The Archivist greets me, and I request information on the case. He sighs, while his dormouse familiar peeks over his shoulder, ears folded back. 'More complex than your usual?'

'Just looking into it. That a problem?'

He holds his hands up, eyes me cautiously. 'Don't get your whiskers in a twist.' He's one of the few folks in the city that knows who—what—I am. Part of getting an access pass. 'Be careful, is all.'

~

The Archivist delivers a box to a study room, and I begin my research. There are dozens of news cuttings mentioning The Taxidermist, alongside pictures of maimed creatures—blinded, stuffed, put on display. I search for Reyn's case, but there are no pictures of the fox. No mention of her at all.

Next, I unroll a city map and circle the landmarks where familiars have appeared, crosschecking them with news reports. Familiars have been turning up dead for almost a year, yet they've only been displayed over the past few months. The Taxidermist is trying to catch someone's attention.

I take a note of some of the cases, then head to the adjacent library building. It's quiet at night—only Nocturnals out and about, who, like me, prefer to be left alone.

In the magical lore section, I find the tome I'm looking for on familiars. Inside, a passage catches my eye: Many believe familiars are both of and not of this world, so that they may see both worlds at once through their eyes.

A lore similar to my own. A connection to the Otherworld. Eyes, to see the dead.

To see better than most.

~

The next evening, I wait in cat form near Reyn's, hidden in a vent, and watch as the courier I paid knocks on her door. Reyn reads the delivered letter with a frown, then quickly leaves. As she rounds the corner where I'm hiding, she freezes. My hackles rise. No way she could see me. But she only stops for a moment, before continuing towards my office. Coast clear, I skirt her building, shift to human form, and pick the lock. Before I go farther, I need to know everything that Reyn knows—because I'm sure she's hiding something.

Her apartment is a disorder of papers and books, stacked unevenly on every surface, nothing that connects Reyn to anything. Then, my gaze lands on the fireplace where a frame sits on display, the only thing not covered in dust. It's a picture of her and her fox next to a woman that looks so familiar. And I realise. I know her—Melanie Jay. Bringing her in for trial was one of my bounties.

I pick up the frame, turn it over, and open the back. A news cutting falls out. 'Necromancer found dead in prison before trial. Melanie Jay's death was reported as accidental, though her familiar was found beside her, eyes removed. In an exclusive interview with the Oracle, Melanie's sister, Lorreyn, claimed the death was the Order's fault. The Order refused to provide a statement…'

A clicking noise comes from behind, a key turning, and I quickly put the frame back. No time to sneak out, so I run to the nearest cupboard and hide inside. Footsteps pass. I take a slow breath. An acrid smell fills my nostrils. And I realise, it's not as dark as it should be. There's a sliver of light behind me. A door. I crack it open and peer down to a basement. Shifting into cat form, I head downwards.

The smells grow stronger. Vinegar, oil, rot. There's death here. I can sense it. Souls lost. Restless.

Illuminated by candlelight, several shelves line the basement walls, displaying glass jars full of bones, tiny hearts, swollen lungs, pale intestines that could only belong to small animals or birds. Or familiars.

A sudden chill fills the room, and I realise I'm no longer alone.

'Enjoying the collection?'

Reyn.

I turn, shifting back to human form. 'You're The Taxidermist.'

'Did you think you were being clever, tricking me to leave you to snoop around like some cunning cat?' She smiles a rictus grin. 'But as I told you, I see this city better than most.' She unfurls her scarf, and I can't help but gasp. Around her neck are dozens of tiny eyes, blinking intermittently, reflecting candlelight like a jewelled necklace. Then she removes her gloves and cloak, revealing arms and shoulders covered in more eyes, moving independently, widening, narrowing. Before all fixing on me.

This is dark magic. Necromancy. I can feel it burning in the air, as unsettled as the restless dead. 'Why have you done this?'

'You should worry more about what I'm going to do next,' she says. 'I wasn't lying about needing your help. I want to see my sister again, the one you took from me. I thought the familiars' eyes would be enough, but they only bring me glimpses.' She raises her arms and the eyes blink in unison. 'Not like your eyes. They're stronger, in and out of the Otherworld. They'll do just fine.'

I scan the space for an escape route as The Taxidermist descends. The upper door is still blocked, but there's a vented window in the corner. The gaps between the metal bars to the street are small, too narrow for my current form. Though, maybe, just wide enough to fit a cat.

# Be Still, Iron Heart

I've always thought that the speckled light that dances between the boughs of trees holds a special kind of magic. A spattering of brightness. Blurred edges. The quiet stillness of a secret kept safe. As I lay sprawled on the forest floor, heart pulsing, I was afraid it would be the last thing I'd see.

~

This forest had always attracted dead things. Locals told me of ghosts and curses reawakened, of wisp-like spirits tempting children inside, of a man cloaked in green, roaming by cover of darkness. And I'd seen the curse with my own eyes. A child who had met the green man had returned with lesions of moss on his skin, spreading far and fast. The family pleaded with me to help, along with a fee I couldn't refuse, paid half in advance, half after I removed the green man's heart and lifted the curse.

So now I walked the green man's way, trees whispering around me, their trunks lacquered with lichen, branches diseased with root rot.

I was headed for its centre, where the oldest tree stood—tall and greying, with roots that were said to reach to the earth mother herself. The further I walked, the darker the forest grew, trees packed so closely together that roots had become exposed forming channels between them, everything connected. It was quieter than it should be for the middle of the day. No birds or insects, just a stillness that seeped into every nook of the forest. A chill crept down my spine. Hairs rising. My hand reached instinctively to my dagger and remained there.

Then, a voice carried on the wind, calling me towards it. I was getting close.

In the clearing of the old grey tree, everything was stone-still. I looked around for the green man, but there was no sign of anything else living and breathing. I approached the trunk slowly. My foot snapped a twig.

The tree screamed in response.

I stumbled back and watched, wide-eyed, as the tree cracked open, splitting down the centre. From it, a man stepped out cloaked in moss and leaves. His eyes were hollow gaps, and his mouth was woven half-shut with vines. I took my dagger out, but the man just let out a strangled laugh and leapt towards me.

Everything happened so fast. I thrust the dagger forwards, plunged it into his sinewy chest. But it did nothing. He only smiled at me with a rictus stitched-together grin and pulled the dagger out, throwing it away into the dirt.

Then the green man was upon me, branch-like arms driving me into the earth. Roots reached up from the ground and wrapped around my legs. One of my arms sunk into the earth below, fingers bending painfully in the coldness. I let out a muffled cry as the green man reached for my throat. Light sparkled in the boughs above and I thought, *this is how I die.*

He lifted his head to breathe in the cool air, savouring my moment of death. Two whispered words hissed in my ear. *Be still.* His mouth was so close to my face I could smell his rotten breath, tendrils of vines stretching outwards from his lips.

It was then that I noticed a pendant around his neck—an iron chain with a green heart enclosed in its centre. Pulsing in beat with the thrumming in my ears. With my free hand, I reached for it. He flinched, held my gaze with those dark hollow eyes, and tried to protect the chain. But he was too late. The heart was in my grasp. I took hold of the iron chain and tugged it free. Another screech reverberated—from the forest or the green man I wasn't sure, but the vines around my legs retreated, nevertheless. Breathing hard, I pulled myself out from the earth and brushed the dirt and debris from my body.

I stood over the man, shaking. His body had turned rigid, face blank and featureless. Moss and fungus speckled his wooden form, life clinging to death. I pocketed the pendant, then, with my dagger, split the wood in his chest and dug into where his heart should be. But his body was only an empty husk.

With the green man dead, I returned to the village. The family were jubilant—the boy's moss skin was healing, and they paid me the remaining fee without question for ending the curse.

It was only as I was walking away from the village that I remembered the pendant in my pocket. Curious, I weighed it in my hands, feeling its soothing warmth. I couldn't help but put it round my neck, and the iron heart rested over my chest, pulsing in beat with my own. Moss bloomed under my fingernails. My mouth itched with a metallic taste.

Something whispered from the forest, and I answered its call.

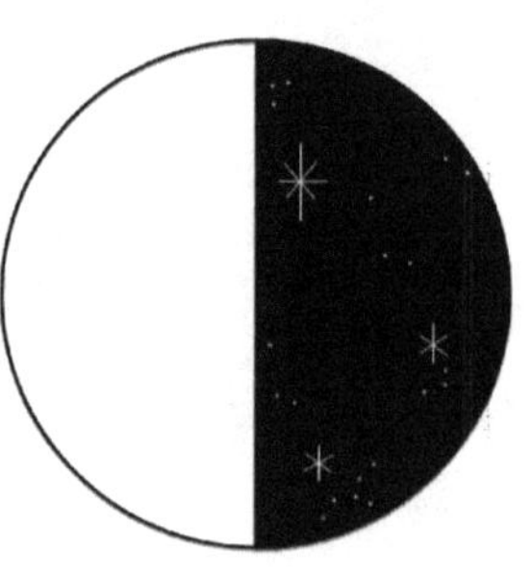

WINTER

# The Fiddler and the Muse

When Magnus saw the advert for the live-in recording studio, he knew it was a sign. The paper was slightly grey, torn at the edges, with the description framed within a red border:

*Recording studio for rent. Live-in option available. Central location above popular bar in the Old Town. Soundproof. Inspiration guaranteed. Length of stay flexible and full payment taken at the end. Serious in-person inquiries only with Bevan Shea, owner of The Muse.*

He took the details and address down on his phone and returned hastily home to pack. For weeks he'd been doubting his musical talents, struggling with his demo. No matter how hard he tried, the notes wouldn't line up. He'd tried mixing things up differently, loop pedals, adding synth, keeping it more trad with fiddle only, and still he couldn't find his sound. Everything came out bland and uninteresting. That morning he'd been about ready to throw his fiddle out the window and give up on it entirely. Then, there on a noticeboard just outside his flat, was an advert that might just be his chance to make some progress. He often had his best ideas when out of his normal routine, so a change of scenery would be perfect. And, with the flexible option, the longer he stayed, the higher the cost, which would be just the type of motivation and pressure he'd need.

So, with his fiddle, equipment, and overnight bag in tow, he left his flat and headed to meet Bevan at the Old Town bar.

~

The entrance to *The Muse* was through a small stone archway which led first to a courtyard beyond with a single tree dominating the space. Despite the central setting, he'd not noticed it before. But then he didn't often come to the tourist areas if he could avoid it, unless he had the odd ceilidh or wedding gig to play. The pub was almost hidden by the tree's gnarled branches and trellises of overgrown ivy. Most of the windows were shuttered over and it looked closed. It was late morning, but he hoped Bevan would be in and that he'd not just come across an old advert.

Above the main door, the sign hung with *The Muse* written in dark crimson lettering with an image of two people dancing in a waltz underneath. Quaint, he thought, and he liked the name—he hoped it lived up to its description.

He walked up to the door and lifted the brass knocker but found it already slightly ajar. He stepped inside and called out a greeting. No answer.

The area was more expansive than he'd expected, stretching back further with a bar at the front and a dancefloor at the back. The furnishings were traditional, with tartan and dark wooden seating, heavy curtains, and there was a smell of whisky and woodsmoke in the air. It was pleasant and welcoming.

'Hello,' he said again, louder this time, and he knocked instead on the counter, peering up the stairway just to the right of the bar. There was a last order bell next to the till, so he set his things down and shuffled behind the counter. But as he was about to ring it, someone spoke behind him.

'Here about the advert?' she asked in a voice that was so soft it was almost musical.

Magnus dropped his hands to his side and spun round. Standing at the base of the stairs was a woman with sharp features peering out from the shadows with a raised eyebrow. Magnus thought she was a woman of contrasts amongst the dark wooden furnishings, skin pale, black wavy hair, a long straight white dress that stretched to the ground and concealed her feet. He'd never been in the presence of someone so striking.

'Ah, hello,' he said again, lifting his chin up. 'Yes. I'm here about the studio. You must be Bevan?'

The only muscle the woman moved was her mouth, which quirked into a slight smile. 'Indeed, yes.'

'Great,' he held out his hand. 'Magnus Irvine, fiddler.'

Bevan didn't take his hand but kept them clasped together in front of her. He noticed she had unusually long fingers with manicured nails, pointed at the ends and painted dark red. 'You already brought your things?' Her eyes moved to his fiddle case.

'Yes. If the live-in option is available, I'd like to take it.'

She smiled a little more. 'Very well, let me show you upstairs.'

Bevan led him up the tight spiral staircase to the second floor. Again, it seemed bigger than the layout he'd imagined from the outside, but then the city had a lot of buildings like that, the front-facing façade only a small part of what lay within. At the end of the corridor, past a row of rooms, she stopped at number 'six' and unlocked it. Inside was a small apartment, but with everything he needed—a bed, desk, wardrobe, kettle, an ensuite bathroom, and a window overlooking the courtyard where the tree bloomed green in the sun. Before he could look around too closely, Bevan opened what at first had looked like a cupboard at the back corner which in fact led to the recording studio. Bevan handed him the keys as he peered inside.

'Fully soundproof,' she said. 'And all kitted out. But if you need anything, don't hesitate to ask. I have an office by the bar, and you can ring the bell if I'm not around. We have ceilidhs here every weekend, which you might hear in your room.'

'Thank you,' Magnus said, taking in the studio beyond. 'And payment?'

'At the end,' Bevan said. 'The rates are fair.'

Magnus nodded and checked the studio equipment. It had everything he needed—microphones, sound systems, an old-fashioned armchair and music stand, and walls covered in foam panels. There was also a large painting on the wall opposite the chair with a golden frame depicting a ceilidh scene. It showed a band playing in the background with only two dancers on the floor, a woman in a white dress, and an older man with grey hair. 'I hope you find lots of energy and inspiration here,' Bevan said, pulling his attention away. 'I've been told this place lives up to its name.' She smiled, revealing a row of perfect white teeth.

Magnus looked at her, momentarily lost in her gaze. 'Yes, I can imagine,' he mumbled, then when he snapped out of it, she was gone, the door shut behind him.

He unpacked everything then organised the studio to his needs. When everything felt right, he picked up his fiddle. He sat and stared at the instrument, tried to play a few notes but nothing came. Frustrated, he moved his papers around, sat in the armchair and closed his eyes. When he opened them again, he was drawn back to the painting on the wall. It was strange—he'd been sure that earlier the woman was facing the other way, but she was now spinning away from the man, a smile on her face. He examined it more closely, deciding that he must have only caught a glimpse the first time. It was a beautiful painting though, and he imagined himself playing in such a beautiful scene, a trill of a fiddle, a couple dancing, a soothing waltz, back and forth, one, two, three, down, up, down. So it would go, and even as the songs changed, the music would blend into the next, and the couple would find themselves dancing the night away.

Blinking away from the painting, Magnus headed back to his apartment for a glass of water. He paused when he saw the window. It was dark, night-time already even though he was sure he'd only been in the studio for an hour or so. There was music coming from down below, a ceilidh band. He'd thought the ceilidhs were only at weekends, and it was Thursday today. He headed down to check—maybe they were just rehearsing. On the spiral staircase he bumped into Bevan, who was holding a basket, her eyes bright with the reflected candlelight from the sconces on the walls.

'Thought you might like some food,' she said. 'How are you finding the studio?'

He peered down, but she was blocking his way to the bar. There was a trill of guitar and fiddle downstairs. 'Good, thank you.'

'And your music? Any progress?'

'No,' he admitted. 'Not yet.'

'Best get back to it then,' she said, her voice with a sing-song enthusiasm to it. She pushed the basket into his hands. 'No time to waste.'

'Yes,' he said, though part of him wanted to watch the ceilidh band downstairs, maybe join in for a jam session. 'I suppose you're right.' Basket in hand, he headed back upstairs, the sound of the band softening as he got to his apartment at the end of the hall. After eating the soup and bread she'd prepared for him, with coffee that tasted both bitter and sweet, he settled himself back in the studio again. He picked up his fiddle and after a few quiet minutes, found himself drawn to the painting once again, imagining the merriment below. But something was odd about it. This time the woman was twisting under the arm of the man, her face no longer looking towards him. Her dark hair had lifted slightly with the motion. Frowning, he leaned in closer and closer and then came a sound. A few notes of fiddle music. He held his breath and listened again. Maybe it was the music below, though Bevan had said the room was soundproof. Then, after a few silent breaths, there it was again. A melody. Just three notes, smooth, mournful, *up, down, up*. He raised his fiddle to his chin, and he played the three notes, *up, down, up*. He played them over and over, again, and again, until they were just right. Then he took out some blank sheet music and scribbled the notes down. He'd found the start of his next song.

'Ha,' he cried out and he could have kissed the painting. 'Thank you. Muse indeed!'

In his excitement, he headed out to his room again, planning to go down and tell Bevan she was right, that this place really was inspirational. But he stopped and squinted at the brightness of the afternoon sun blaring through the window. He blinked at the light. Had he fallen asleep? There was no sound coming from below anymore—the ceilidh was over. On his desk was a new basket of food, the old one removed. Bevan must have dropped it off. There was hot soup inside, fruit, some oatcakes with cheese, and flapjacks that smelt like treacle. A decadent offering. He found he was suddenly ravenous, so he ate first, then as he was tempted to head downstairs to speak to Bevan, the three notes trilled in his head again. He hummed them to himself, as though expecting the next note to come. He felt like he was on the cusp of it, so he headed back to the studio, locked the door, picked up his fiddle and played the three notes, his eyes again on the painting. Now the dancers were bowing to one another, the man with his foot forward, and there again, a soft tune and a bass, two more notes, making five, *up, down, up, up, down*. A smooth melody, the bow moving easily along the minor key, creating the start of a beautiful, mesmerising song. Something wasn't quite right though—it sounded too sad, too sombre, so with another glance at the painting, he added an extra note to give it a hopeful twinge at the end. He scribbled them down, then ecstatic, played the tune over and over until every note he played was perfect, and he couldn't get the melody out of his head.

~

So it went, Magnus watching the painting change, weaving their movements into notes so that soon he had a whole page of a song. He played it over and over until his arms ached, and he could think of nothing but the musical notes, and even when he closed his eyes slightly to rest, the song was in his dreams, and so was the painting, the couple waltzing back and forth to the music he'd created. When he opened his eyes, not thinking much time had passed, the painting had changed again, hands held then not held, one foot forward then the other, dress twirling—*and were those hooves beneath the woman's feet?*—and the man in the painting now had a beard, but he was bowing and laughing, and Magnus could almost hear the man's voice, and he too was humming the melody as they moved, *one, two, three, up, down, up.*

Every time he left the studio, the light in his apartment had changed, whether sunset, sunrise, afternoon, he lost track of the difference. There was always another basket of food, and so there was no need for him to go downstairs. As he ate, he glanced at the unmade bed, noticing dust on the bedside drawers, and tried to remember the last time he'd slept. But he couldn't. For a brief moment, as he stared at the dust, he snapped out of the reverie, realising that the last time he'd looked outside the leaves had been green, and now the tree outside was a rusty orange, leaves falling from twisted grey branches. He stood to go to the door, catching a haggard reflection of himself in the window touching his face and finding hairs had grown across his chin and jaw. He rubbed them absentmindedly, then thought of the fiddle there, and a new note came to him. He forgot that he was going to leave, and he darted back into the studio, looked again at the painting, and began to write and play the notes, a constant thrum and trill, of *ups and downs*, and *one, two, threes*, over and over, repeating the song, in his dreams and in his waking, because he quickly became unsure of the difference.

~

One afternoon, Magnus finished his song, ending on a high note that left room for the next song to follow on. He looked at the painting, which now showed the dancers embracing, and he wanted to reach out and hug them himself. He had to tell Bevan he'd finished, so, fiddle in hand, he wandered down to the bar. Bevan was waiting in the seating area with a smile. It was snowing outside, and he caught his reflection in the frosted glass again—salt and pepper long hair, dark circles under his eyes, a grey beard. How long had he been here?

'You've finished?' Bevan asked him.

'The painting,' he said distantly, lost in his image. 'The muse…the song.'

'I'm glad you found it so inspirational in the end,' she said. 'Are you done with the studio now?'

He frowned. 'Yes, I suppose I must have stayed longer than I planned. What do I owe you?'

She stepped towards him, and she looked exactly the same as the day they'd met. How long ago had that been? Surely the process of finding his song hadn't been so arduous as to turn his hair prematurely grey. 'Can I hear what you created first?' Bevan said, her voice lilting, lifting up slightly at the end of the sentence.

Magnus was pulled back under her gaze, and he felt a well of pride and a desire to prove himself. He followed dutifully as Bevan led him slowly to the back, where a stage was set in the corner for him. As he walked across the dancefloor itself, with its tiled wooden flooring and shiny surface, he noticed it looked a lot like the scene from the painting. Everything with the stage, the band, the woman dressed in a white dress, and him, now about to sit and play with his fiddle. It felt right.

Taking a deep breath and smiling distantly at Bevan, who stood in the centre of the floor, Magnus began to play. Bevan bowed at the first *up, down, up*, and began her waltz as the song progressed. Magnus was transfixed by her. He played as Bevan danced around the floor, moving as if his music gave her energy, her feet clip-clopping on the solid wood, and she lifted her dress and twirled, and Magnus saw that her feet were hooves, like the woman in the painting, clip-clopping with the *up, down, up*, and the *one, two, three*, and she twirled, and he watched, and found he could not stop watching, and when the song ran out of notes, he just began again, and so did she, so he kept watching, and she smiled and laughed, as if his song were the best thing she'd ever heard, so he smiled and laughed too, as he played until his fingers bled, then even when the strings started to snap, he kept playing, and when the melody was broken, he hummed the notes himself, until finally when the last string broke, and his throat almost dry, Bevan stopped dancing and walked forwards, hands no longer clasped at her front but held up, outstretched, sharpened nails pointing towards him, and he was so tired, so exhausted that when she slipped a nail against his throat, and let it slide into flesh, he did not, and could not, resist her. As the blood ran down his neck he imagined the pulse of his heart, *one, two, three, one, two, three*, and with her mouth on his throat, and his eyes roving back, with an *up, down, up, up, down, up*, the melody of the painting played in his mind, and he hummed it until he could no longer.

# Woman of Ravens

The grey woman sits on the rock, hunched over and frail. A cowl of silver-white hair wraps around her shoulders, illuminating the moorland clearing like a beacon in the night.

Euna approaches, head bowed in deference, an offering clutched in her hands. She's careful not to hold the rosemary too tightly—not to let any sprigs break off and scatter on the heather below. An earthy smell suffuses the air, peat and smoke, and something else. Something sweeter. The mountains towering on the edges of the valley make it seem as though the landscape is smiling, and she's walking straight into its cavernous mouth. But this is what she knows she must do if she is to understand her nightmares. Every night it's the same.

*A shroud in her mind. An all-consuming darkness.*

A breeze tickles Euna's cheek as she stands at the edge of the rocky outcrop.

Soft as a whisper, a voice comes. 'Tell me what you seek, child.'

Euna steps closer and places the bundle of rosemary at the foot of the rocks. She bows her head but says nothing.

The grey woman leans forward, looking upon Euna. Her face is wrinkled and pallid, but her eyes are as bright as sunrise. 'Do you not speak, girl?'

'I…' Euna feels her throat constrict. 'I am unsure of the customs.'

'You are here, and yet you do not know the customs?'

'I only heard you could help me,' Euna says trying hard to keep the wavering in her voice at bay. 'My mother never told me how, except that I must bring a gift. I don't have much, but I hope this is enough.'

A pause. The grey woman nods slowly, her eyes fixed on Euna's face. 'Very well. Tell me what it is that ails you.'

Euna's mind races with the images of her dreams, but she takes a deep breath and tries to piece them into a coherent description. 'In my dreams, there is a darkness. In it lives a creature, a raven, I think, writing in a black cloud.' The words are spilling out fast now. 'But its eyes are empty, and it screams so loud, as if in pain. Every time it does, I try to run toward it to help, but the cloud consumes us, and under my feet, all that remains are piles of bones and ash.'

The grey woman says nothing as she reaches for the bundle of rosemary. Euna holds her breath as the other woman cradles the flowers in her palms. Then—somehow—the bundle is on fire, though Euna didn't see a spark, nor a flint to light it. The grey woman holds it without concern, the flames seemingly harmless. It burns with a pleasant tang, and Euna is reminded of something she can't quite place.

As the flames die, the grey woman blows across the bundle. From the embers comes smoke. So much smoke. A dark cloud, filling the air. Euna's heart quickens with a sudden desire to flee. To run. She backs away, but the woman reaches with charcoal-stained hands and holds her wrists tight. The frail woman is stronger than she looks, fingers rough and spindly, still warm, nails digging sharp into her skin.

*A scream in the dark. Smoke in her lungs. Tears in her eyes.*

*Run.*

*Run.*

The smoke surrounds them, and its acrid taste sticks in Euna's throat. She coughs and splutters, staring up at the woman, willing her to end whatever this is. Maybe Euna got the offering wrong. Maybe she came to the wrong place, and this woman is not the one from the stories—but the other kind, the kind she's been warned about. Witches and curses, demons and darkness. She tries to pull away again, but the woman's grip is too strong. Unyielding.

And then, in the growing gloom, the grey woman shifts. Her eyes become beady black, her nose pointed and sharp, like a beak. Her grin is wide as black feathers sprout from her skin like petals blooming, so fast, they make a fluttering sound as they extend over every inch of her body.

Euna recoils as the woman shrinks and shimmers into the form of a raven.

As her wrists come free, she falls back and tries to crawl away. But she's not quick enough. With bright beady eyes, sharp and keen, the creature soars forward like an arrow, plunging beak-first into her abdomen.

Euna yells, and claws at her stomach, trying to find the bird. It's no longer there. Instead, there's a twisting pressure, as if something is burrowing into her gut. Digging deeper and deeper. Her chest tightens with each movement, and she can no longer breathe.

She has experienced this feeling before. Breathlessness and pain. Loss and confusion.

Somewhere deep, in the back of her mind, she remembers.

~

Euna was walking through the market, hand-in-hand with her mother and grandmother, when the men arrived. Yells of confusion filled the street as woman after woman was rounded up and seized. When her mother spotted the men, she dropped her basket filled with rosemary—the scattered sprigs falling like teardrops—and lifted Euna into her arms. Her grandmother, unable to run with them, urged them to leave without her.

'Take Euna. Run. I'll catch up. Just run.'

She cried, wrapped her arms around her mother's neck, lay her head against her chest, felt her racing heart like a drumbeat. Her mother sang to her as she ran, a song about a smiling valley, and the kind old woman who lived there. Her lilting voice almost drowned out the wails and screams. Almost. But the men were too cunning with their watchful eyes, blocking every escape.

Euna did not understand. Not when they tore her from her mother, kicking and screaming, telling her it was for her own good. Not when her grandmother and mother were dragged away.

Not when they tied them to a wooden pyre.

Some of the men held books and read verses aloud as townspeople were gathered in the square. One man, dressed all in raven-black, eyes narrowed, stood before the pyres, torch in hand, and proclaimed to the crowd, 'This town has been poisoned and must be cured. Do not stand in our way, and you will not be harmed. Those who are innocent will be spared.'

Euna was spared the burning herself—mercy, the men said, for not bearing the mark.

But she was not spared the horror of it as she watched her screaming family burned.

A black cloud engulfed the town, blotting out the daylight, the smell of burning so thick, it clawed at her throat and made her sick. And once the screams finally stopped, she slipped away from the men, away from the darkness, and ran.

Euna ran and ran until days and weeks and months all bled into one.

With each passing moment, she pushed the memories from her mind—the screams, the burning, the raven-man, the shame—until she forgot it all and only a shroud filled her mind.

She sought refuge where she could. Took jobs here and there, fled further north, until she found her way to the valley of smiles. At night, she was still haunted by the dream of a dead-eyed raven. Of bones and smoke and screams. And when she woke, Euna would think about stories her mother had told her. Of the grey woman in the smiling moor, who could help people heal, find meaning in their dreams, or guide them to their truth.

And so, Euna had gone there, to seek her wisdom. To help her understand her nightmares. To help her remember again.

~

When Euna wakes, her body is curled into a curve, arms clutching her stomach. She stands up slowly and looks around. The grey woman and the rocks are gone, and she is alone in the quiet, smiling valley. Her eyes adjust to the dark and she notices a dark ring of strange flowers before her. The plants look like heather, though she has never seen flowers with withered black petals and pale white stems. Nor has she seen growth in this odd pattern, mimicking where the rocks had stood moments before. Cautiously she approaches it.

'Hello,' she whispers into the night.

Only silence responds.

Her stomach twists again, and she lifts her shirt to her midriff. The skin underneath is smooth, untouched. A sudden spasm grips her, then a wave of nausea. She retches. Something sharp sticks in her throat then prods at her tongue. She coughs again and, with a splutter, dislodges the object. She pulls it from her mouth, and it comes out bristled and wet—a single black raven's feather. She examines it in the light of the moon.

She looks again at the circle and steps into it, walking on the withered heather, and it sounds almost like the crunching bones from her dreams. A light breeze dances in the air, tinged with the sweet familiar smell of rosemary.

As she breathes it in, her body twists. A sudden force pulls at her limbs, stretches her out, body and soul. But there is no pain. Only a sense of lightness—as though this is how she was always meant to be. Feathers prickle along her face and shoulders until her arms become wings. Her feet curl into talons, and with a final twist, she jumps into the air like a plume of smoke.

As she soars into the night, a fluttering of wings echoes beside her. They soar together in a flock above the smiling valley, and into the clouds. Euna glides across moors and mountains, watching the wilderness below. For a time she goes here and there, with her flock and the dark of night keeping her safe.

Then, one day, she spies smoke rising from a town below. She dives and lands upon a spire, watches as cloaked men roam the streets. In the distance, a woman is being dragged and tied to a post, crying silent sobs, her hair thick with blood and dirt. Euna flies down and lands by her side, a twisting in her gut.

A new sensation, an urge awakened.

As a cloaked man approaches the post with a torch in hand, Euna caws loudly. Summoning her flock, she rushes him, talons and beak outstretched. A scream fills the air, but it does not come from the woman this time. Euna savours it, lets it trill in her mind, pushing all other thoughts out.

For she is now the woman of ravens, and she has no mercy for unkindness.

# Nuckelavee Winter

'The waves are so still,' Sara says to me one morning. 'It's a bad omen.'

I look up from my breakfast. 'How so?'

'When the Sea Mither sleeps, the frost seeps,' she recounts. 'But it's too early for winter.' She walks over to the kitchen window, arms hugged around her chest.

When I first arrived on the island, Sara's stories were what drew me to her. Her voice soft and lilting like a spring breeze, with the power to transport you to other worlds. But her words today have an edge to them, her voice distant and vague. Is she worried I'll leave when winter comes? This was only supposed to be a summer fling after all, but summer soon turned to autumn, the seasons changing as quickly as the tides. I go over and wrap my arms around her, kiss her lightly on the cheek. 'If the snows come,' I say, 'we can keep each other warm.'

But she doesn't reply or look at me—her gaze is still fixed on the view outside the cottage. On the beach, the old standing stones watch the water as silent guardians. They've always unnerved me. Beyond them, black waves ebb and flow. Sara's right. I've never heard the sea so quiet.

I wake in the middle of the night and find Sara gone. The front door hangs open sending a whistling breeze through the house. I pull on a waterproof and wander outside to look for her. A light snow drifts across the landscape, the cold night air smelling of seaweed and salt. Snowflakes melt on my cheeks like teardrops. *Too early for winter.*

As I cross the beach, a shadow emerges between the standing stones. At first, I think it could be a horse. But on its back is the torso of a man with translucent sinewy skin, arms so long they drag across the ground. Its head lolls to one side. A single red eye traps me in its gaze. My breath catches in my throat.

Sara steps out from behind the creature, a taut expression on her face. I want to yell out and warn her, but I can't seem to speak.

'I'm sorry,' she says. 'I wish we had more time. But winter always demands its sacrifice.'

She steps to the side as the creature comes towards me. It exhales a long rattling breath, and the snow suddenly swirls around me in a whirlwind, blotting out the light. The piercing cold roots me to the ground.

When the snow clears, Sara and the creature are both gone. I try to move, to shout out for her, but it's like my body has turned to ice. All I can do is watch the water. A crescent moon reflects on the sea in a Cheshire Cat grin. Waves cackle on the pebbled beach.

The Sea Mither is awake again.

# A Song, Remembered

When I was ten years old, I almost drowned in the sea. But as the waves crashed overhead, pushed me into the currents, an old woman appeared from the watery depths and dragged me towards the shore. As she took my hand, cold bony fingers tight around my wrist, she hummed a song so strange that I never forgot the melody. A beautiful lilting tune, only slightly dulled by the churn of the waves. In the blur of saltwater, her face was obscured, though her eyes were round and glasslike. When we were safe again, she pushed me away, and locks of her silver hair shimmered like glitter in the water until she disappeared into the murk below.

Back on the beach, people gathered all around me. My parents fussed and I told them there was a woman in the water, that she'd saved me. That they needed to help her too. They only looked at me, faces pale like they'd seen a ghost, then they wrapped me up with blankets and towels and told me not to go back in the sea.

Later, on the same holiday, I saw the woman again. I was combing the beach at sunset by a lighthouse on the island's peninsula and its beacon momentarily lit a figure moving through the water. The old woman appeared slightly above the waves and looked at me with those same glasslike eyes, silver hair floating on the surface tangled with seaweed. She stared at me, and I stared back, dropping the shells I'd gathered to the sand. After a moment, she put a finger to her lips and disappeared back under the water.

We returned to that island every summer after until I was grown up, though I never saw the woman again. Sometimes I thought about putting myself in danger to see if she would come back, but every time something stopped me. The memory of her song would return to me and, as I'd hum the melody to myself, my reckless thoughts would be gone.

~

It's almost a lifetime later, a long time since I've last been to or near the island, when I wake up from the strangest dream, left with the memory of the woman and her song. And I know with a sudden clarity that I have to return to the island, if only to see it for one last time.

The place is quieter than I remember when I arrive—an island almost abandoned with half-empty houses, and buildings falling apart from weather or disuse. I rent a cottage by the lighthouse beach and spend every night there looking out to sea. Still the woman doesn't appear.

One morning, a heavy haar falls over the island, and as I look out to the horizon, a bright light shimmers in the haze beyond. I walk into the sea, uncaring of the cold stinging water wrapping itself around my old bones. I float there, relaxed, always at ease in the sea, and listen to the stillness. After a while, an odd noise comes from somewhere. The sound of voices and the crash of waves, echoey as if they come from below. I take a deep breath and dive under the water to listen again. The sounds return along with the hazy light shimmering in the water ahead of me. I follow it, swimming with the currents, until I no longer know what is up or down. It's strange, but I feel like I can hold my breath forever. So I do.

I don't know how long I've been swimming for, only that as I finally reach the light, there's a tangle of limbs thrashing above me. Someone trapped in the suddenly strong currents just below the water's surface. A young girl, her body being pushed away from the light. Without thinking, I kick up towards her and reach out a hand. My hand wraps around her wrist, and I pull her away from danger. To calm her, I hum the song from my dreams, from the old woman in the sea, the one that has haunted me all these years. When she's safe, I let her go then retreat to some rocks to watch from a distance. The beach is much busier than when I left it, and the haar has lifted. Tourists crowd around the almost drowned girl as her parents take her in their arms, wrap her up with panic on their pale faces. Faces I recognise from a long time ago, though it's impossible. Confused, I dive back down and search for the shimmering light again, but I never find it. Though it seems I can swim under the waves forever and never tire, from the surface to the bottom, no matter how deep, without coming up to take a breath.

I don't know how much time has passed, as I'm drifting aimlessly in the water, like a jellyfish in the deep, when a bright shimmer reflects above me. The lighthouse beacon from my childhood. I follow it and swim to the water's surface. There, in the bay, I see the girl I saved looking out from the beach, her hands full of shells. She drops them and stares at me, and I stare back for a long moment, finally understanding. I put a finger to my lips then dip back below the waves, where I'll remain, humming the song from the place I almost drowned once, and the place that, in the end, I've returned to rest.

# Two Faces of Winter

Cold wind bites into my cheeks and I know that it signals the change. The stripping of leaves, the spattering of dew-frost, and the startling brightness of a sun drooped low in the sky, all mean my days of walking the land are limited.

I know it's coming every year, yet the moment still seems to sneak up on me—so much am I enjoying roaming mountains in spring, visiting beaches in summer and watching as life blossoms all around. Though I no longer measure my time in years, each term I serve feels different, every cycle offering something new and exciting. Often, I find myself forgetting the winter months that have come and gone—as if my mind has blotted out the memory of such desolate moments.

This year, the impending cold is like a slow tug, and I prepare myself for my body to stiffen—for the battle of the seasons to wrench me away from my youthful freedom. As my body turns frail, I take a final pilgrimage to the mountain and sit upon the craggy rocks that will form my throne for the onslaught of winter to come. I steel myself for my long hibernation, knowing that even if there is pain, at least the warmer seasons of freedom that come after will help me forget.

I close my eyes. My mind drifts in and out of consciousness, as the darkness and freezing winds batter me from every direction, until I'm no longer here nor there.

Something disturbs me. A crunch of frozen bracken. I force my eyes open, and gaze across the land. A clouded haze encompasses the space around me. But I can sense I'm no longer alone.

'Who comes here?' I whisper, my breath a mist.

A pale figure appears. 'It is time to drink from the chalice, my queen.' A woman's voice. She blinks up at me, her hands holding my golden artefact towards me—the one I drink from in the spring and summer months, to fuel my rejuvenation.

An uncomfortable knot spools in my chest. How can she pick it up? Only I have that power. Who is this imposter? Red hair, woven with intricate wildflower vines, frames her neck and shoulders. Something tells me she is known to me, though I cannot place how.

I look around again at the frozen landscape, feeling the icy bitterness of it deep in my bones. 'It is too early. Winter is not over yet. Leave me be, whoever you are.'

'Ah.' The woman smiles. 'But I'm here to offer you an opportunity. Don't you want to end your torment early? To have a longer spring, a longer summer?'

I frown at her. 'Yes, it *would* be great if I could just decide to get up and end this, but that is not the way. The length of the seasons is a thing that cannot be altered.'

'But you could change that, if you decide it.'

I shake my head. What does she mean? 'Who *are* you?'

'I understand, you don't remember me,' she says. 'But you can trust me, I only want the best for you. Come, don't you want to be born anew? Drink!' She pushes the chalice closer. Air bubbles move on the icy surface of the water within, threatening to escape with the lightest touch. Maybe it really is almost time. How much I crave the warmth. How much I want to feel the soft earth beneath my feet.

A slow wind whistles in my ears, and I search for any hint of sun. It is still low in the sky.

Winter isn't over.

And it is forbidden to drink from the chalice too early. I take a slow aching breath. 'It is not yet time.'

The woman cocks her head. 'I'm sorry my queen, but now *is* the time.'

'I am tired. Go away,' I say, my voice rising like a rumble of thunder.

Her eyes dart around. 'Please, just listen. You cannot enjoy being stuck here, the pain of being frozen in one spot, hardly able to move for months on end. It is a cruelty no one should have to endure.'

'No.' I sit up to get a better look at her and my bones creak. 'I don't enjoy it particularly.'

'A cruel fate,' she says and shivers. 'So you must drink. Drink and you'll be renewed, refreshed. This is a gift, only to be given to you, my queen.'

If it *is* a gift, then there would be a cost. There is always a cost. If I drink now, winter will end early. Then I may not have energy enough to keep the warmth flowing when spring comes, and just like that the seasons would be disrupted. No, I will not be tempted. This is a balance I have kept from time immemorial, and I will keep it still. Why is this woman trying to get in my way? 'Who do you think you are, meddling in things you cannot possibly understand?'

'Ah, but I *do* understand.' There's a strange gleam in her eye—like a spark waiting to ignite. 'We are more acquainted than you can know.'

I search the woman's face again. She looks younger than me, her skin luminescent against the fiery redness of her hair. There's a hint of familiarity, but it is vague and slippery. 'I don't care who you are. We're done here.' I close my eyes and hope she'll go away.

But she only laughs. It is a tone I recognise. 'Alas,' she says. 'You have thwarted me again.'

I open my eyes slowly. She is standing so close to me, like her figure is a reflection in glass. The illusion is shattered, and I remember who she is.

I am her, and she is me.

The fogginess fades and memories of our past interactions flood into my mind. My other self, the form I take in the spring, appearing before me like a mirage, tempting me from my slumber early, trying to break the sacred binds laid upon us. And so, I know what comes next. She will make me forget, until we're forced to engage in this whole episode once again. 'One day I will remember your attempt at treachery,' I tell her.

'And one day you'll fall for it. Then we will be free from this curse.' She sighs. 'What a shame I cannot force your hand. Alas, maybe next time. But until then…'

She waves a hand in front of my face, and I hers.

For a moment my hand hangs out in the air, withered and wrinkled, pale and blue. The movement hurts, as if my bones could break at any moment. I look down at the chalice at my feet, the water inside completely frozen over. It is not my time yet.

A flurry of snow begins. As it lands on my skin, the coolness of it courses into my muscles. It stings with a familiar kind of suffering. But it feels right. This is what I must endure.

The world becomes a void of white.

~

Birdsong rings in the air. The bleating of lambs echoes in the fields below, while the sun warms my skin. My chalice of gold lies next to me, appearing as it always does when I wake.

I take a long drink and stretch out my limbs, until they no longer feel like stone. It feels as if I have been asleep forever. As always, the long months of cold are a blur in my mind, the ache in my muscles the only memory of my torment. And even that pain is starting to subside.

I stand and look down the valley where hints of green are already starting to appear. As I gather my hair over my shoulder and weave it into a braid, the last hint of silver-white fades into red.

# SPRING

# To Gut a Fish,
# First Gather its Bones

Aggie had survived more than a lifetime of worries and woes when she heard the dreaded song of the Marool across the sea and knew that her last remaining grandchild had been taken from her. There was an inevitability in the song of the great fish—for many years, it had haunted her, as her husband, sons, daughters, and grandchildren had set out to sail and one by one, failed to return. For a long time she'd been deemed too frail to sail upon the water, her bones too weak for the journey. Now, she'd been left behind on the slowly withering island with only the memories of her stolen family as company.

~

The old tales had always warned of what lay in the depths—of the dangers of sailing further and further from shore, to cast off nets and bring in more treasures or riches from the deep. But it took too long for the islanders to listen. Too many boats scuttled, crews drowned, and too many bones of the dead drifting up on shore.

Every time a tragedy befell a ship, the islanders saw taming what lay in the sea beyond the horizon as a challenge, so they built the next boat bigger, stronger, more seaworthy, and made offerings to the Sea Mither for a safe passage. But the sea, as with seasons and time, cannot be tamed, even by the fearlessness of youth.

As the sea stilled on the night that Aggie heard the Marool's fateful song, two days since the last ship had sailed out with her grandson on board, she looked out over the water to see the distant glow of the great fish's lure drifting upon the horizon. It was a soft blue light casting across the waves.

Before her grandson had left, she'd implored him to stay behind—asked him at least not to be foolish, not to join a hunt if one was begun. For the islanders had woven nets large enough to catch a whale, and stone-tipped spears sharp enough to fight it. Aggie knew that it wouldn't work. The Marool was too cunning for wood and rope.

When the boat didn't return, Aggie knew neither the weather nor the stormy seas were to blame, but the great fish himself. And there and then she vowed she would get her revenge.

~

None left on the island had seen the Marool, though Aggie had always believed the old tales. How else could so much be told of a fabled creature if none had witnessed it in the first place? Perhaps the Marool was malevolent once, roaming the seas, his crest of flames a soft glow to aid travellers as they cross dangerous waters. Perhaps the island folks had angered him, and now he sought vengeance. There was nothing in the old tales about the reason he had become such a monster. As is the nature of such tales. They're old. They miss important details. But in the stories told to warn youngsters from swimming too far from the coast, the Marool was a hideous beast, a fish the size of a whale with razor—sharp teeth and a stare as dark as night. He was said to have a shining lure that hung between his myriad eyes making his gaping maw look like it glittered with treasure. Then, if any were swimming deep enough under the waves, they might see the lure and swim unwittingly into his jaws, eaten alive merely for the curiosity of youth. All that would remain would be the discarded bones that washed up on the island's shores.

~

Every morning, Aggie limped along the eastern beach, her walking stick in hand, collecting washed-up bones. The remains were clean of skin and sinew and barely distinct from driftwood, not even in shape. Indeed, most islanders told themselves that's what they were—hollow and pale white wood, made smooth by the sea. Though none would touch them, nor look closely enough to be proven wrong. When they saw Aggie gather the pieces each morning after the tides receded, she may as well have been invisible for all the attention they offered. They muttered under their breaths about her then went on their way. It didn't stop Aggie, though. If anything, it added to her resolve.

Aggie had long gathered the bones together in a sea cave near that eastward shore. She had tried, at first, to reconstruct their many parts so she could lay them to rest. But in death, bones are too similar to distinguish a pattern of belonging. Sometimes, she thought about turning them into something beautiful as a way to respect them—she had been a carpenter before arthritis withered her fingers and left her knees stiff and weak. But, as she looked at them laid out every day, the whisper of the sea nearby a reminder of what had taken them, she could not decide a purpose. So, the bones lay in indistinct piles, a shrine to the sea and the danger within. The piles grew and grew, until soon every crevice of the cave was filled with the remains of the dead.

~

Weeks after hearing the Marool's song, Aggie wondered if she would recognise her grandson if he washed up on the shore. She would be combing the beach, and a hand would reach up from sodden sand, skeletal fingers, broken and half missing. Maybe she would recognise the one that was broken as a child, that still held the scars of injury. And she would collect them nonetheless and await the rest of the body.

In reality, when the latest bones washed up, she could not distinguish any feature that set them apart nor tell whether they had come from her grandson's boat or one from months before.

The wreck of his ship did, however, eventually wash up amidst the flotsam and jetsam. An array of splintered wood, the whole structure gutted and destroyed by the great fish. Everything discarded, broken, except for those who had lived aboard it. Their souls belonged to the Marool.

The islanders gathered the wood from the coast and built a ceremonial bonfire to remember the dead and pray to the great Sea Mither. There was a song the island folks sang for lost souls at sea, and Aggie imagined it as a counter to the Marool's own tune. Though, she imagined the great fish hearing their mournful ballad and not feeling fear, nor worry, but instead believing them weak. The islanders sung of great tragedy yet never learned from their past mistakes—every time, they sailed right into the jaws of the Marool, unprepared and foolhardy. Aggie was not so naive. Not after losing all she had to live for. Besides, the Sea Mither must have left these shores a long time ago. There was no one left for the islanders to pray to.

After, an island meeting was held, a gathering of all who remained, and Aggie sat quietly at the back. Again, the options for the next sailings were discussed, and it was the same as it always was. A hunting party, a bigger ship, more supplies. But Aggie believed that the bigger the ship, the bigger the target.

She raised her hand slowly and when the island leader called upon her, she said as unwavering as she could, 'You cannot continue like this. We must try something else.'

The islanders turned their heads but didn't give her much heed. After a quiet pause, the conversation continued again with plans for new weapons and nets. Losing patience, Aggie stood up, walking stick in hand and found her way to the front. She cleared her throat, and eventually they gave way to let her speak.

'We must find a way to trap the Marool, trick him, blind him, cut off his lure so he can no longer see,' she said. 'And we can't do that with the ships we're using right now. They're too large, he will see them coming from a mile away.'

'So your plan to defeat the monster is to use less force?' the island leader said, humouring her, at least.

'Yes. We must be strategic, precise. A smaller crew on a smaller boat. And it must be made of something stronger. Something that can withhold a fight with the Marool and not be crushed in his jaws.'

'What alternative do you have in mind?' the leader asked, with a frown. 'There is nought more on this island but wood, sand, and stone, and I'm *sure* you're not suggesting we throw stones at the creature?' There was a murmur of laughter, but Aggie didn't rise to the provocation.

She stood her ground. 'If we are to defeat the monster, we must think smarter than it. Fight not to defeat his brute force, but to counter with something different. It is the only way.'

The island leader shrugged and looked around. 'An alternative suggestion has been made by Aggie here. Anyone volunteering to head out to the waters with nothing but a rowing boat and your wits?'

'I will go,' Aggie said. 'If I must.' The islanders laughed at that, and when none volunteered to support her, they waved her away and returned to discussing their original plan. Aggie sighed and returned to her seat, listening distantly. More trees would be cut down, rope woven, and a crew gathered to man the next journey. Fragile materials and even more fragile minds, Aggie thought, realising her suggestions had been futile. No one would listen to her, a frail grandmother in mourning. Maybe she could use it to her advantage. It would guard her from their view as she set about her counter plan to hunt down the monster. Just as the Marool's beautiful lure would tempt a weary swimmer or sailor,

Aggie could use her perceived weakness to her advantage. If she had to, she would set out to fight the Marool herself, and none on the island could stop her.

Aggie returned to her cave that night and sat with the bones as she looked out the cave's mouth to waves lapping on grey sand. And as the full moon rose high in the sky, casting its light across the pale white bones around her, she realised. There *was* more than just stone and wood on this island after all.

Aggie knew the dead wouldn't mind. The Marool had tried and failed to fully destroy the ship and regurgitated what it could not consume.

So, she began to arrange their bones in a different way—the forgotten and restless dead with their mismatched parts. First, she fashioned armour with the same care she had once crafted furniture. Wove femurs together to create guards for her aged legs, helping her stand upright without effort. A helmet she made from fingers tied side by side with leather and old fishing net, with two jaws hooked together to protect her face. Around her torso, she created a cuirass of ribs, curved around her shape so that she became twice her size. She felt powerful, fearless.

Sometimes, she worried the other islanders would try to stop her, but when she roamed the beach gathering the new bones, washing them in seawater, none paid her any mind. She was just a mad old woman with a penchant for dead things. They continued with their plan, and she continued with hers.

It was the rowing boat that took the longest. A vessel made from smoothed and hollowed out skulls and vertebrae, an oar made from shoulder blades and leg bones. Every night she worked on the structure, using anything she found discarded on the beach to strengthen it, to make sure it would take her where she needed to go.

Finally, Aggie crafted a long dagger from a sternum, sharp and light. In the handle, she carved the names of her fallen family, then as she held it towards the sea it shone as silver as a lure in the moonlight.

"Sea Mither, defy me," she whispered her intent to the waves. "I'm coming for him."

In her bone-clad armour, and her boat made from the remains of the dead, Aggie set out at sundown to seek the Marool's lair. The sea was calm for her, and she breathed in its scent. The only sounds were the waves sloshing against her boat, and her bone armour creaking with each stroke of the oar. She didn't look back at the island as it faded into a dot behind her.

She had been rowing for half the night when she finally spotted the soft light of the Marool in the distance. She rowed slowly, careful not to attract his attention, until her boat was above the source. He hadn't sensed her yet. But he soon would.

Leaning slightly over the edge, she took her oar and swished it in a round motion. She sang a soft song as she made a whirlpool in the waves, a mix of the Marool's and the counter song the islanders sung. His light moved upwards. Aggie steeled herself. She dropped the oar and picked up her dagger instead, moving carefully to the very back of the boat. When the Marool raised his ugly head above the water, his crest of flames glowing bright in the sky, teeth as sharp as glass, the light of the lure gleaming azure on her boat made of bones, Aggie shouted a battle cry and called the Marool forwards.

The Marool opened his jaw wide and let out a long gargling shriek. Aggie looked at the chasm within, the chasm her family had once faced and succumbed to. And she smiled, baring her teeth beneath her helmet of woven jaws. She waited a few long seconds as the Marool moved to swallow her and the boat whole. The force sucked the water down. The boat tipped forwards. She locked her legs in her armour and held onto the stern of the boat, then when the Marool was close enough to touch, she leapt forwards, dagger in hand, and cut off his glowing lure in one precise swipe. In reflex, the Marool's jaw snapped shut and the sound of teeth breaking against the boat of bones echoed amidst the thrashing of water. Aggie fell back and held her breath, imagined the faces of the islanders if they could see what she'd done. The Marool flailed blindly, the boat now stuck in his jaw, and Aggie, having done what she'd set out to, let herself fall into the cold stinging sea.

Her bone armour dragged her downwards with the lure, still casting its light in the greyness in a luminous blue. She watched as it entangled itself with a jellyfish swarm, and as the lure's light faded, the jellyfish themselves became beacons, blooming into vibrancy. A trade had been made, awakening new light in the dark. They followed her descent to the seabed, lighting her way. The Marool followed, sinking down and down, the boat of bones trapped in his jaw and throat, the light in his crest dying. His scales shimmered silver then dulled, eyes blinking out one by one. The creature sang in a warbled sorrowful echo, but Aggie felt no pity for him. She had done it. She'd faced the monster that had taken her family.

When all was done, Aggie lay in the sand at the bottom of the sea next to the Marool, cradled within her bone armour, and jellyfish dancing in the moonlight. As the water wrapped itself warm around her, she let out a breath and closed her eyes.

~

In the new tales, soon to be old, it is said that in deep dark waters the Marool still lurks, half-living, half-dead, sunk into the seabed by the bones of those it killed. Around it, jellyfish swim with their new light, adorned by the Marool's lure. And, it is said, that an old woman made of bones lies beside the monster she slayed, a shrine for those lost and forgotten at sea, avenged, and finally laid to rest.

# The Lighthouse Seer

The boy arrived at Elenya's lighthouse a day before her first Rites, sailing through the haar as if drifting over clouds. She watched his approach eagerly from the lantern room. It had been months since she'd seen another soul, except for the occasional seal or seabird seeking solace on her lighthouse cliff.

When the boy was close, she descended the spiral staircase and walked barefoot onto her rocky island. The boat was moored at the small pier, bobbing on black waves. She took a deep breath and prepared herself. The air tasted of seaweed and salt, as it always did. Like home. She picked absently at the scales under her fingernails, from the fish she'd been preparing earlier.

Her visitor eventually stepped onto land, carrying a wooden chest with a brass lock. He was dressed all in grey with hair the colour of night and eyes like silver. He couldn't be much older than her, seventeen or eighteen.

'I brought an offering.' His voice was hoarse suggesting a long voyage. 'You're the Lighthouse Seer?'

Elenya nodded. 'You're a day early.'

His lips parted slightly, his breath escaping in a wisp-like mist. 'Oh. Will you send me away?'

She frowned. Tomorrow, people would arrive from all over the archipelago to seek her Rites. Her job was to give them guidance for the months ahead, and they would bestow offerings in return—supplies or trinkets. She wanted to know what was in the boy's chest. 'I'll be busy with preparations today,' she said, then closed her eyes and inhaled slowly, feeling the change in the wind. Clear in her mind she saw it—a whirl of water, roaring of waves, thrashing of rain. 'A storm will come tonight,' she said half surprised at her words, the vision over. 'You should stay here, there's a spare room.'

The boy looked enthralled. Not many people got to witness a Seer's sight. 'I'd be grateful for your hospitality, Seer. I'm Shea.'

'Elenya,' she said before thinking, forgetting that she was supposed to have given up her name. She glanced around, expecting to see one of the Brethren appear and scold her for breaking the rules.

'I'm honoured,' Shea said. 'I'll keep out of your way then.' He made towards the cottage, but Elenya hesitated. It had been a long time since she'd been around anyone, never mind someone her age.

'Fish!' she shouted.

He turned. 'Sorry?'

She scrambled for the words. 'Do you like fish?'

He smiled. 'I eat little else.'

'Then join me for dinner later. I'd be glad of the company.'

'And I yours.' He disappeared into the cottage with a nod.

Elenya headed to the lighthouse to continue her preparations. When the Brethren arrived tomorrow, they'd expect her to be ready. She lay the Seer's map on the table in the circle room. It showed every island of the archipelago, half the land scribbled out as the sea had taken it. Where was Shea from? Or did he always live on his boat?

She stared at the map for a long time, straightening the edges, running her fingers across the contours, trying to memorise every part. At its side, she placed a bottle of fish oil, seaweed paste, and a bowl of sea glass she'd collected over the months: oil to show fish stocks, seaweed to map safe sailing routes, and sea glass as a luck offering.

Her preparations complete, she returned to the cottage and started a fire. As the sky darkened, the predicted storm began, with battering rain and whistling winds. Shea joined her, and she served salted fish and seaweed soup. As they ate, Shea told her of his journey—it had taken him six weeks to find her. He'd had to stop at various islands to ask for directions, though he said little about where he was from. She asked him what was in the chest, but he wouldn't tell her yet.

'What's it like when you use your powers?' he asked after dinner.

The storm was in full force now. Its rumble echoed through the walls making it feel like they were underwater. She shivered. 'Like a memory, but more vivid.'

Shea held his hands in front of the fire. 'What did you do before becoming a Seer?'

She looked at him, unsure what to say. 'I lived on an island.'

He nodded slowly. 'With your parents?'

'Yes.'

'Any other family?'

Elenya thought about it, but she couldn't remember. Why couldn't she remember? 'I…I don't know.'

'And what did they look like, your parents?'

His eyes. They were so familiar. 'I don't know.'

Shea put a hand on her arm, and she jumped at his touch. 'It's okay,' he said. 'I'm here to help.' Then, he pulled the chest over and unlocked it with a brass key. She shuffled back, suddenly worried what it might contain. But he only took out a sleek grey coat.

'Is that your offering?' she asked.

'It's more of a returning. Because it's always been yours, Elenya.' The way he said her voice sent shivers across her skin. 'I'm glad you still remember your name. That's a good sign.'

'I don't understand.'

'When the Brethren stole you to take advantage of your gift, they made you forget,' he said. 'But they're not your brethren. I am yours, though. Now that I know it's really you, I'm here to free you.' He held out the coat.

Hand shaking, she reached out and touched it. A vision flooded into her head, like a tidal wave engulfing her senses. She was swimming, further and further, into the deep. And she felt at home there, in her sealskin, dancing beneath the waves, singing in her ancient tongue. She knew of the seasons and the way of the waves. It wasn't the knowledge of the land-walkers. The ones that had ruined all that is sacred and beautiful.

The fog was lifted. She looked up at Shea, her brother, her friend, her true brethren. 'I remember.'

# A Change in the Rain

The rain smells different by the sea. Petrichor mixed with a salt-tinged stench. I didn't used to think about the rain, or how it smelt. Nor stand beneath a cloud, imagining what it would feel like if the skies suddenly opened above me. I yearn for the touch of water, even if it would likely be the last thing I felt.

In reality, when the rains come, we hide. Boards over windows, leaving barely a thin gap to peer through. Stormguards over doors in case tendrils of the rain and rising seas try to break their way inside. Ma makes hot tea and soup on the stove, while I light candles and stock the fire. When night falls, I sit in the dim light and pick at the dry skin around my fingers and cheeks while we wait for the storms to pass.

The translucents had the right idea about the rain and sea, I think. The figures that decided not to fight back when the weather turned against us, allowing themselves to simply melt away into nearby rivers and seas. They are pale things, the translucents, not quite ghosts, not quite like us, forms pockmarked with seaweed and sand. When it rains, they still slither out from the sea and linger on land amongst the storm, faces stretched and featureless. Often, they stand outside the houses they used to live in—like Pa does outside ours. I recognise him from the way his body tilts slightly to one side as he stands swaying in the rain. Sometimes he comes so close to our door that he knocks against the wood, a *tap, tap, tap* that lingers with the pattering of rain and hail. Once, I put my eyes right up to the gap, looked straight into his face, and found I couldn't look away. I stood trapped there until the rains finally stopped, and his figure slipped back to the sea and into the waves. When I told Ma about it afterwards, she hushed me, said I'm only imagining things—all I'm seeing is the onslaught of the storm, and all storms pass, eventually.

Sometimes, on clear days, I stand on the beach and wonder what would happen if I just walked into the sea and never stopped. Would I turn into a translucent like Pa? Would it hurt as the water stripped away my skin and dissolved my features?

Maybe this is what the world intended for us anyway. Why else would the rain itself have turned so against us?

~

I'm sitting on the beach one evening, staring out at the water, when the Rain Bell rings. In the distance, up at the cottage, I hear Ma calling for me. Around town doors and windows slam and clatter, everyone preparing to hide from the oncoming storm.

I'm about to stand to head back too, when I notice something in the water. A bodiless head, floating on the surface like a buoyed jellyfish. I stare at it, and it stares at me. As it tilts to one side, I realise it's Pa, watching me. We stay like that for a while, unmoving, until I can almost imagine the features of his face again.

It's only when a single drop of water lands on my neck that I look up and see the whorl of black clouds gathered above me. When I look back to the sea, the figure in the waves is gone, so I turn and sprint to the cottage. I don't tell Ma about the raindrop when she pulls me inside and scolds me for being late. We rush to put up the rain defences, and it's the same routine as always. As it always will be. I find myself wondering how this can be any better than giving in and becoming a translucent—hiding from the inevitable, not taking action, simply preparing, and waiting for the next storm, time after time.

Later, when Ma is asleep, I inspect my neck by candlelight. The skin where the raindrop fell not only glistens but stretches, translucent, beneath my touch.

~

This storm rages for four days straight, and every morning, the patch on my skin has spread. When a tap, tap, tap comes at the door one night, I rush to the gap in the window and look out again to find Pa. I don't even try to pry myself away this time, and as the rains surge, I find myself mirroring his movements, seeing expressions in his featureless face I've not noticed before. A smile, a laugh, a mouth shaping voiceless words. When the rains stop, and he melts away again, I realise I can't remember having taken a breath for hours.

~

When the patch has spread to the size of a limpet shell, I prod a finger slowly into the jelly-like skin. With only a slight amount of pressure, it slips right through into my throat. A deflating hiss of hot air comes out from the translucent gap, though when I remove the finger, the skin rearranges itself and the hole disappears. I prod it again a few times, attempting with each to suck in a breath through the gap, though with every effort, I almost choke on the dry air. When I look out to the water, I finally understand what it needs instead. What I need.

~

I know Ma wouldn't come with me if I asked her. Even if I told her that this is no existence, hiding inside, never changing how we live, pretending like the earth hasn't already moved on without us.

So, when the next Rain Bell rings, I ignore it. Instead, I walk alone as far along the beach as I can, away from town, and sink my feet into the soft sand. The rain when it comes smells different again. Saltsweet, rather than the stench I usually notice. And when the skies finally open, I walk into the sea's embrace and never look back.

# The Fisherman's Wish

Standing on the westward shore, the Fisherman looked out across the water, eyes peeled for any movement. He had heard that a rare fish could be found in the water nearby—a once-in-a-lifetime catch. So far it had evaded him, despite his best attempts. Along the rockpools he attached floating traps and laid nets so that they covered the length and breadth of the bay. He sat on his boat with his sturdiest fishing rod, used up his best bait, but still, there was no sign of anything rare or otherwise lurking in the watery depths.

In a final attempt, he bought a special lure from a trader—one that was said to attract any creature of the sea. It was a strange thing and unlike any lure he'd seen before—egg-shaped and golden, only to be used in the dark. When the moon shone on its surface, it emitted a fire-like glow as it bobbed slightly weighted below the water. The trader had said the light would confuse and disorient the fish, attract it like a magpie would be drawn to silver and shiny things. He'd never heard of a fish that liked shiny things, but at this point he was prepared to try anything. Every Fisherman has a nemesis, and this fabled creature was his.

So, as the moon rose pale in the sky, he waited and waited, watching the golden egg bob up and down in the ebb of the grey sea. As the sounds of the ocean grew still, his eyes became weary with the watch and his body slumped into sleep.

Some hours later, he was awoken by a distant splash. Neck snapping up, he stood so quickly that he knocked his stool over behind him. Cursing himself for falling asleep, for missing the movement, he stared out into the gloaming. He was about to give up hope when a tail bigger than any fish he'd ever seen appeared and slapped the water just where the lure lay. And then, an almighty splash and thrashing began, and the gleam of the lure blinked out of existence, as if swallowed whole. *It worked*—the lure had caught him his rare fish. His heart raced as he ran forwards, whooping, into the water until it soaked him up to his midriff. He hardly noticed the coldness of it as it soaked his skin, adrenaline warming every inch of his body. He started to tug on the rope of the net, to pull in his catch, when something peered out of the water, its form distorted by the netted cage. Round moon-like eyes, skin silvery-pale, hair as black as seaweed. Not a fish, but a woman. With his knife held out, he ran forwards to release her, to confess his mistake, to beg her forgiveness. But then he saw the tail swishing behind her and the reason for her silvery appearance—her body was covered in scales. He froze and stared at the strange creature.

The woman stared back for a long moment before lifting her chin to the sky and opening her mouth. She let out a gargling sound at first, and then she began to sing, a soft, lilting melody. The Fisherman was struck still by the beauty of it, as memories flooded into his mind, happy, calming ones awakened by her song. His mind drifted back to childhood, to days spent swimming in the bay, jumping from the rocks, scouring pools, searching for shells and hermit crabs in the depths, throwing flat stones into the water and watching them skim across it. When she stopped singing, an empty coldness crept in, and he was brought back sharply into the darkness of the night that now felt like a shroud. 'I recognise your song,' he said, even though he could not explain it. 'Can you speak?'

The woman tilted her head a little. 'I should not speak to your kind,' she said, her voice as soft as her song, more cautious than cruel.

The Fisherman blinked, already wishing he could hear her voice again. 'Why not?'

'I have heard you are dangerous,' she said, and she moved in the water in a mesmerising motion, her webbed fingers pressed flat against the netting as if in surrender. 'Though, if you set me free, if you rescue me, maybe we can talk more?'

The Fisherman hesitated, watching the whirl of the woman's fishtail in the water, of her body shimmering as bright as any quartz. 'If I rescue you, free you from the net, what's in it for me?'

The woman considered him, then she smiled, close-lipped. 'It is said that should a land-dweller help one of our kind we must grant them a wish.'

'There are more of you?' the Fisherman asked, eyes darting across the water. 'What are you?'

She gargled a noise in the back of her throat, an almost-word he recognised from old tales and stories.

'Ceasg?' he whispered.

She smiled. 'Yes. At least that is what land-dwellers call us in their tongue.'

The Fisherman thought of the tales of the Ceasg, creatures with strange powers, and the ability to whisper wishes to the sea. 'So if I help you, you will grant me anything I want?'

She nodded, her fisheyes widening into a pupilless chasm of grey. 'Yes, once I am free you may ask me for one thing, and so it will be.'

The Fisherman considered his options. A wish now, whatever his heart desired, or he could keep her. What would the rest of the town say if he showed up with her instead? She could be his star catch, a treasure from the deep, the rarity he'd been searching for. People would pay good coin just to see her. The magical Ceasg—half fish, half woman. He could be rich beyond any imagination—a haughty goal for any fisherman. And when he'd made his fortune from her, he could set her free and then ask her for the final wish. This way, he wouldn't have to waste a wish on becoming rich. He smiled, stepped forward, knife in hand, and instead of cutting her free, cut the base of the net and wrapped it around her.

'What are you doing?' There was a choked panic in her voice as she flailed in the water, trying to escape.

'You are too rare a creature to set free,' he said, dragging her roughly to shore.

~

The Fisherman took the Ceasg home to his cottage and tied her up in his tub, though with her fishtail she couldn't go far anyway. After she'd tried to escape with no success, she merely sat still in the cold shallow water, crying. Though there was sadness in her voice, to him it sounded like the most beautiful song—even her tears were special, streaming down her face like melting silver.

'Please, set me free,' the Ceasg said to him as he was brushing the sand and sea from her hair, preparing to show her off to the world.

'Not today, my treasure,' he said. 'I'm not yet rich, and besides, I've not decided on my wish.'

She looked at him unblinking, a hunger in her eyes, and said, 'you are a monster.'

'And what does that make you?'

She let out a long breath that came out fluttering through the gills on her neck. He shivered but found he could not look away.

'If you are going to keep me here, could I at least have more space?' she asked. 'My scales are itchy and I can hardly breathe. I need to stretch my limbs, or I will die.' Her face softened as she lifted her bound wrists. 'No one will pay to see a dying creature.'

The Fisherman couldn't help the pity creeping in, like a stone sunk in his stomach. As her grey stare bore into him, he had a sudden desire to do as she asked, to make her happy—and so, he set about making a pool for her in his garden, reasoning that it would also make it easier for visitors to see her.

The Fisherman spent weeks building a wooden container that he gradually filled with water—bucket by bucket from the sea. He then took the Ceasg outside, her body as light as driftwood, and placed her in the pool. At first, she swam back and forth, bashing against the sides as if in protest, then when she ran out of energy, she sunk to the bottom and stayed there, her moon-like eyes gazing at him from the murk. He pushed the guilt away and used the leftover wood to make a sign which he hammered into the sandy earth at the front of his cottage—an invitation to the town to finally visit the fish-woman. He travelled to the fish market, the local inn, and the town square to spread the word. By the time he returned home, a whispering crowd had gathered outside.

Taking a coin from each visitor, he let the townspeople into his garden. At first, the Ceasg would not come up out of the water, but then he tempted her with food and fish, and eventually, she started to sing. Her voice floated in the air, enchanting and beautiful, casting its spell over everyone gathered. Just like her song had enthralled the Fisherman, the Ceasg had become a treasure to them all.

As the days and weeks and months passed by, many returned over and over again to glimpse the magic of her, to hear her song, to sit and watch as she glowed silver under the moon. Soon, word spread to neighbouring towns and islands, and travellers were coming from far and wide to witness the marvel of the Ceasg. The Fisherman turned no one away until all the chests in his house were overflowing with gold —more fortune than he knew what to do with. He had become rich without wasting a wish, just like he'd hoped.

At night, after sending the visitors home, he would sit outside with the Ceasg and speak to her of his success, of the visitors that had come that day, of his new dreams to travel away from the island. And he told her that he wished to take her with him, that they could be happy together, become richer and richer, and go wherever they wanted. She would float and listen silently, responding occasionally with a smile or a wistful sideways glance, before singing him to sleep under the stars.

One night, after a day of visitors, she persuaded him to take her for a swim to the sea, promising she would not go far. He found he could not refuse. He took precautions though. With a rope tied tight around her waist, he carried her down to the westward shore and let her swim in the bay for a while, dipping and diving under the waves, a smile so wide on her face that he couldn't help the warmth he felt at seeing her happy—a brightness shimmering across her that he'd not seen in months. Afterwards, as the moon rose full and golden, like the lure she'd swallowed so long ago, she sang her lilting song, transporting him back to his happiest memories, of the sea and the shore, and the day they'd first met. At the end of her song, she swam up to him, put a hand on his and spoke with her silver tongue, 'I so miss the open water. You are rich now, beyond your wildest dreams. So won't you set me free?'

And that was how the Fisherman realised he had fallen in love with the Ceasg. Over the months, he had cared only for her, become mesmerised by her beauty. She was his only company, his confidant, but she was there against her will, and what sort of life was that? When she asked if she could leave, he felt such a sadness because he couldn't imagine his life without her. He didn't want to let her go. She was a treasure and was worth more than all the gold in the land. But what use was a treasure if it wasn't truly his? With a shame that tugged on him like an overfull fishing net, he knew that he could not keep her forever. Not unless she chose to stay.

'If I set you free now, would you stay?' he asked, a hope in his heart that maybe, deep down, she felt the same way.

But the Ceasg only looked upon him, her face scrunched up in disgust. Then she said with such sharp cruelty, 'no. Not if you were the last creature alive in this world would I stay with you. Not if you begged me, asked me to be with you forever, I would never. I would not.'

It felt like the Fisherman had been harpooned in the chest. How could she, after all this time together, not want to even give him a chance? Did she feel nothing for him? He could not fathom it. For he loved every part of her. Her song, her beauty, her eyes, the way she brushed her fingers through her hair, the way she looked out towards the sea and whispered her secrets into the wind. He didn't want to live without her.

And, he realised, maybe he didn't have to. Because he still had one wish. He stepped towards her, knife in hand, and cut the rope between them.

The Ceasg saw her chance and quickly began to swim away, but he shouted out to her. 'Wait! My wish. You must grant me my wish.'

She turned and swam back to him. 'Very well,' she said. 'What is it you desire?'

The Fisherman stepped forwards and dropped the rope. 'I cannot be without you. I wish to be with you forever.'

The Ceasg looked up at him, the same hungry expression in her eyes she'd often had back in the cottage. 'So it will be,' she said, and her mouth stretched into a grin. It was the first time that he'd seen her true smile, the one she'd hidden in her sideways looks and sad expressions. Now her smile was powerful and inhuman, and it widened and widened until her jaw cracked open, revealing row upon row of razor-sharp teeth and a dark maw within. The Fisherman recoiled and tried to run away, but his feet were twisted in the rope he'd used to tie her with. He fell back just as the Ceasg towered over him, her mouth wide, her song suddenly ringing like a warning in his ears. The last thing he saw as the Ceasg swallowed him whole was the moonlit sky, a gold beacon in the dark suddenly snuffed out.

~

The Fisherman did not remember what happened next, only that he woke up in darkness, a slosh of something like waves all around. He called out for help, pushed against the strange soft walls that now encased him. He looked around, searching for any hint of where he might be—trying not to think about the beach, of the Ceasg and her smile, and what had surely just been a nightmare. Then he spotted something, glowing in the distance. A golden egg—the lure he'd used so many years ago. He ran towards it and gripped it in his hands, smoothing its surface. He held it in the cavern within and it shone a warm glow around the distorted walls. He pushed his hands against the walls again, and they rippled in response. Then there was a rumble somewhere in the distance, followed by a song he recognised—the song of the Ceasg, muted as if heard through a shell. Or, through the hollow stomach of the woman he loved and had wished to be with, forever.

# The Woman of Thorns and the Honeycomb Queen

Deep in the Otherworld, in the land between life and death, the Queen sat on her honeycomb throne as visitors from all the realms presented their gifts. Nectar, mead, silk, gold—always the same every season, year on year. An endless cycle. And the Queen would have to sit and be gracious, even when all she wanted to do was return to her room where she could be left alone.

Everyone knelt and lay the offerings at her feet one by one, and they'd make their requests of the Queen—a healthy harvest, thriving businesses, true love, or a happy family. In return, she'd carve off a fragment from her honeycomb throne and present its magic to them, feeling herself weaken with each cut. 'Your Queen is most grateful,' she'd say. 'May your home be protected, your days be bountiful, and may all your wishes come true.'

And so it went as the days wore on. Her throne gradually became depleted of honey while her energy waned, until the final visitor of the week approached. The woman was unlike anyone the Queen had ever seen—she wore a long yellow silk dress, and her face was covered by a mask of thorns. But before she could make her offering, the Queen's guard stepped between them, a poison-tipped sceptre in hand. 'You're not on the list,' he said, holding the weapon in a point towards the woman's chest. Behind them, the Queen's wings whirred in a drumbeat thrum. 'The week's festivities are over,' the guard added.

But the woman of thorns was not perturbed. 'You must have time for one more offering. For I have come so far, and I wish to present a different kind of gift,' she said. 'A performance. A dance, for my Queen.'

The Queen's eyes lit up, and she waved the guard away—he stepped back, though still kept a watchful eye on the visitor. 'And what do you seek in return?' she asked the woman of thorns.

'Only to spend a moment in the company of my Queen and hopefully make her smile. That is enough for me.'

The Queen couldn't help but smile at that. She'd always loved to dance, and it had been a long time since she'd been allowed to attend any ceilidhs or even had the energy to. The realms took so much from her. 'Then please, begin.'

The woman of thorns bowed low, then began her dance in rhythm with the Queen's buzzing wings. As she waltzed, ribbon-like vines stretched from her arms moving in mesmerising patterns, while flowers bloomed in her hair—sunflowers that had always been the Queen's favourite, even though she had forgotten that until now. In her final act, the woman of thorns reached into her pocket and presented a handful of pollen-like dust. With a swift pirouette, she turned and blew the pile straight into the guard's face. Before anyone could react, he collapsed. Moments later, as the pollen swirled around the throne room, the rest of their company followed suit, falling one after the other into a deep slumber. All except for the Queen, who rose from her throne, eyes darting to the doors as if expecting someone to burst through them and call this all a big charade. But no one else came. 'Who are you?'

The woman of thorns removed her mask. 'Please don't worry my love, I've come to rescue you.'

And as the pollen swirled in the air, the Queen remembered. The masquerade of the Otherworld lifted. So long she had been here, between life and death, doing her captors' bidding, pretending to be a Queen, letting herself wither while the realms around her flourished. So long she had spent her days bound by the whims of all but herself.

No more.

'You found me,' the Queen said, stepping down from her throne, gazing at the woman from her past life. Though the memories were still vague, she remembered she'd once loved her, long ago, in the land above, where time passed by as easy as the clouds, with days and nights, and weeks and months, and moments to cherish, and people to love. A place without wings or magic, but where she could dance freely without someone watching her every move. 'I've been waiting so long to be released from this prison,' she added.

The woman of thorns smiled. 'I travelled from above and below in search of you, but now it is time to come home. Things will be clearer then, your mind will become as sharp as thorns, as it once was.'

As the fog started to clear in her mind, the Queen felt a warmth in her chest, as sweet and pure as honey. She took the hand of the woman of thorns, and together they fled the Otherworld, leaving only a pollen trail and a sleeping kingdom in their wake.

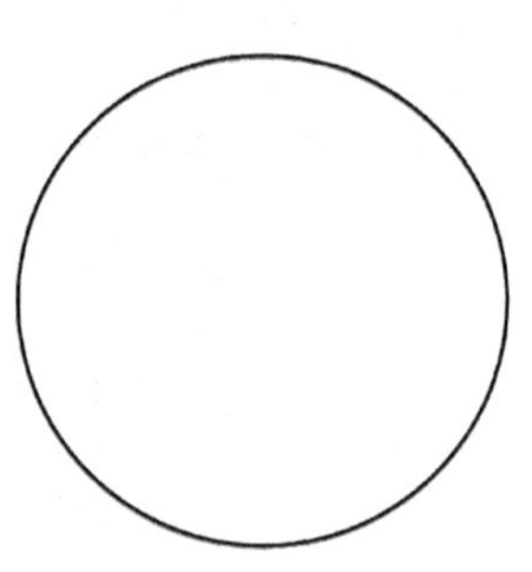

SUMMER

# The Loneliness of Water

The first day I saw her, she was just a movement in the corner of my eye. A passing shadow hunched over on the beach amongst the flotsam and jetsam. *She's not real, was all I could hear trilling in my mind. She can't be real because I'm the only one left.*

In my fear, and stubbornness against hope, I stayed stone still, staring instead into the gloaming and haar like I did every day at dusk, not going too near the water, and trying to pretend I did not see the movement to my right. But I could hear her. The pebbles crackling like a whisper with each step. Her rasping breath in rhythm with the waves. I heard a story once, when I was a child, about a woman they called sea witch. If she was not perceived, then she could not be real—at least, that was what the stories had claimed. What would happen if I looked? Would that make her real?

A splash sounded next to me, and my curiosity won. I turned. But she was already gone. A ripple on the waves, fragments of seaweed floating on the lonely blue. I walked to where she'd been last, though never as far as the water's edge, and sunk feet into sand. Beside me, was a faint web-toed footprint that was too large to be a seal or otter. But when the waves came in, it melted into the sea and salt, gone forever.

As I turned to head home, I found a small pile of debris. It was organised in a way so as to look purposeful, almost like a nest. Tangled fishing line. Shards of rusted metal. Ripped cloth wipes. Bits of plastic from the old world, relics that would survive longer than those who made them. Things that didn't belong on the beach. I took out a bag from my backpack, gathered the pile up, to take home.

~

I chose my current house for its height away from the water, but still with easy access to the beach. I never could have afforded something like it before everything—a spacious five-bedroom cottage, half-modern, half-restored, with a large garden for growing vegetables, insulated walls, wood-burning stoves, and a balcony and a hot tub that looked out to sea. The latter was a luxury that lay empty now and housed old fishing rope instead of chemically treated water. I placed the small pile from the beach in there and pulled over the cover. On the balcony, I looked out to sea, a distant hope that I might see a boat or a light, or any sign of something other than the endless water. Even the sea witch again. Instead all that kept me company were layers of clouds rolling across the horizon.

~

I couldn't help but return to the beach, wait in the hope I'd hear the sea witch again. And that this time I'd be brave enough to look. I found myself scouring the beach, searching for signs of her. Sometimes I found her mounds, the remnants of things not meant to be in the sea. I'd gather them up to store and sort through later, and then I sat in the same spot, and I'd wait.

Finally, after weeks of sitting, and waiting, I built up the courage to look. When I heard her first—a splash as the tides rolled in—I stole a glance. And I saw her, real and clear as day. She stopped in her tracks. Crouched low, body hunched, face hidden under her knots of hair. She stayed like that for a long time, so still that I started to question if she was just a mound of seaweed, washed up to shore. If I wanted so bad not to be alone that I was seeking company where there was none. I stayed like that, watching the mound until the tide came in and washed her away. Though the pile of objects she'd gathered remained, and I dutifully took them away and stored the pieces at home.

After some weeks, of collecting and observing, I started to gather my own piles nearby, and then, once the sea witch had left her offerings, I'd take them all away with me. I thought that one day they would run out, but while the piles always grew smaller, they never completely went away. Soon my house was filled to the brim with pieces of broken and lost things. Not that it mattered, I had the rest of the village to fill if I needed to—empty houses of those who lived here in the before times. Soon, instead of the sea, it was the houses that stored the memories of the dead.

~

The sea witch started to leave me gifts next to her mounds. Sea glass, pebbles, beautiful shells—natural talismans from the deep. And so, I began to mix the gifts with the broken things, turning the junk into something new. Woven wall hangings. Mosaic mirrors. Flowerpots. Jewellery. Anything I could fit back together again—things that reminded me of the beauty of before. Of moments and things lost to the end of the world.

I wove a bracelet from old fishing wire, attached a piece of sea glass in a charm, and brought it back with to me to the beach, earlier than the sea witch usually appeared, and left it carefully where she liked to pile her things. Then I sat and waited for her to come. As I did, I thought about going into the water to look for her. Considered dipping my head down under the waves to see if she was lurking there, somewhere in the dark depths of the stinging cold. But I'd not set foot off land since the waves had taken everything and everyone from this world and spat me back up like unwanted debris, left behind. Even as I thought about touching the water again, I felt a chill run through me and felt dizzy at the idea of it.

Eventually, the sea witch did come out of the water. And this time, she didn't hide. I watched as she crawled up the beach, towards the pile and took the bracelet in her hands. She turned to me, and I did not look away. For the first time, she saw my face, and I hers. And it was a beautiful thing.

She was not human. But nor could I find the right words to describe her. Creature, witch, goddess—none seemed to fit. She was just her. Radiant in the setting sun, skin luminescent, glistening seaweed-hair flowing so long and so thick that it could have been growing from her back and arms and legs. Her eyes were like dark pebbles, round and black – but they were also kind, and when our eyes met, I found I could not look away. For so long I had not been seen. For so long I had wondered whether I was cursed to be invisible forever. To be perceived after so long was like a reawakening, a stirring in my gut, and I yearned for more.

I smiled at her and raised a tentative hand in greeting. She flinched a little, then sunk down to the ground again. Though, she was still holding the bracelet and her round eyes were just visible amidst her flotsam form. So, slowly, I tapped my wrist where a similar bracelet of silver was hooked in place—something that had belonged to my mother, whose face I'd long forgotten. The sea witch tilted her head a little, lidless eyes wide.

Then, she wrapped the bracelet around her hand and the corners of her mouth twitched upwards into a slight smile, gills fluttering on her neck.

I stepped closer towards her and sat cross-legged where pebbles met the sand. She was hesitant at first, but then she did the same. We sat like that until night fell, and the moon shone luminous on her skin. Then, she slunk back into the sea, and though we'd spoken no words, it felt like we'd shared a lifetime of thoughts.

~

Later, as I looked out from the balcony to sea, dark clouds hung ominous on the horizon. A storm incoming, bringing with it the high tides and thrashing waters. So, that night I slid the storm-guard boards into their runners along each door and locked the shutters on every window to keep the outside out, and as the wind whistled through the cracks, I made mushroom and kelp soup, heated on the wood burner stove. I sat up almost all night, remembering the storms from before, and worrying about the sea witch as the sound of the sea roared and the wind rattled. I fiddled with one of the pebbles she'd left me, one with a small hole in the middle. A hag stone that I remembered was said to help you see into the magic of the otherworld. I was scared to look through it though, in case it showed nothing changed, only the version of the world where I was alone.

While I awaited the morning, I busied idle hands by weaving a cord for the stone and lay it over my chest as a pendant. Somehow, it was a comfort, this little piece of the sea witch that she'd left for me. I still thought of her as the sea witch, for how could she tell me her name, the real one that must exist beyond the stories? That night, as sleep finally took me, I dreamt of swimming underwater, searching for something in the depths, as a shadow followed me but never quite caught up.

~

In the morning, wreckage mottled the beach as if the whole sea had been sick and thrown all it had to the shore. Old fishing nets, plastic containers, metal cylinders, and endless piles of seaweed, twisted and knotted with broken things. All our efforts those past weeks suddenly seemed wasted, that our little haven had been contaminated once more. There were dead things too – birds caught up in nets. Fish that had washed to shore—dead before they drowned on air, it was hard to tell. A baby seal, skin blotchy and spongy lay quiet as if sleeping. I buried them first. A smell of rot filled the air as I dug, and began the clean-up, half hoping for the sea witch to come, while also hoping she would not have to see the devastation—that I could clear it up before she did.

Then, something moved in amongst the mounds of waste. It would have been easy to walk past. Easy to walk past and only see the remnants of a storm. But as I walked towards it, I knew it was her. My heart hammered against my chest, worried that she wasn't sleeping either. That she was like the seal.

Her body was curled up in a foetal position, all wrapped up in an old net, skin grey and faded, scales flaking. The luminescence gone. I knelt down and pulled the net away from her carefully, touched her arm. Her skin was cold, but her chest moved, gills fluttering. She was breathing, but only just in a slow quiet rasp.

'Hello,' I whispered, my voice hollow and strange for I had not used it in a long time. 'Can you hear me?'

I'm not sure if I imagined the whisper back, the slight nod of the head in recognition of me, but I knew I couldn't leave her on the beach to drown amidst the debris.

She was lighter than I expected, and I carried her slowly up to the cottage. I set a fire in the living room and lay her in blankets beside it. The space filled with the scent of the sea and the sound of her shallow breaths. As she warmed and watched the flames, I heated water on the stove then placed kettlefuls in the bath until it was full enough. She didn't protest as I helped her up and lifted her into it. She just sunk down into the water, curled beneath the surface, her hair stretching out in wisps all around her as if encasing her in a protective cocoon. After a while, she turned and blinked up at me, big round black eyes glistening beneath the water. Then, she blew out a series of bubbles from her gills and mouth, and as they bubbled on the surface a sound came from the depths, a voice, distorted but soft, in varied tones.

I smiled and mouthed. 'Do you have a name?'

She tilted her head at me, then blew some more bubbles up to the water's surface, as she waved a motion with webbed hands. It was a beautiful sound, hearing what may have been her name, though I'd never be able to repeat it in my own voice.

'I'll leave you to rest,' I said, and stood up. I didn't know what to do, or what she'd want, but I left a towel on the edge of the sink and pointed to it, mimicked wiping my arms and hair. 'If you need it, for when you're ready to leave the water. Only if you want to.'

I had no idea if she understood me, but something in her gaze told me she did. She gave me a twitch of a smile, then curled up again beneath the water, in her dark-haired shell.

~

As the days passed, the sea witch and I learned to communicate in our own ways. Though I spoke—and it felt good to be saying words out loud to someone, whether she understood them or not—we talked more in motions and other sounds. A hand wave to show directions, as I explained the parts of the town to her, showing shapes, and buildings. When she was able to walk again, with one arm in mine, and a stick in her other hand, we walked up and down empty cobbled streets together, and she'd touch plants or weeds growing between the cracks, and I'd whisper the words for them: daisy, dandelion, clover. And she'd smile and make a movement with her hands as if she was repeating the shape of the words. I liked the shape of dandelion best, the word in her hands like she was casting a spell. Often, birds would fly past or above us on our walks, the world now theirs more than mine, and I'd name them for her as they did. When a pair of lapwings flew by with their distinctive song, instead of mimicking the word for it, she made the slow rising *peewit* sound, a whistle in her throat, with such accuracy that I couldn't help my surprise and wonder. She enjoyed that, and from then on as birds passed, she mimicked their sounds as if she was taking their voice, only momentarily, to repeat their music and magic to me. I wondered what her words for things in her world were, the things she saw in the sea on the beach, or along the coast. Did the way she spoke her words sound different under the sea?

She was fascinated too by fire, if not a little cautious. I pointed up at the solar-powered bulb of one of the town's streetlamps that was still working and made a flashing movement with my hand. Then, later, I did the same with a candle and she stared at its flame for a long time, her finger hovering so close to it her scales glittered with the reflection of it.

When I showed her my studio, of broken things made new, of the nettings turned to clothes and blankets, of wire used to tie driftwood together to make sculptures, of plastic made into mosaics and furniture with sea glass details, she smiled so wide I finally saw her true smile. She had three rows of teeth, and canines like a seal, though it was neither threatening nor ugly. I knew she wasn't dangerous. That she wouldn't hurt me. She moved past me and almost danced around the studio, touching the things I'd made, from the things she'd collected or left me as gifts.

Every time she smiled after that, I felt a warmth in my chest, the same kind I used to feel when I was younger as I swam in the sea as the sun shone down. I'd not felt that way since before the seas rose. I'd forgotten the beauty of the water and only remembered my fear. The loneliness of it. But maybe it didn't have to be a lonely place anymore.

In the evenings, we'd sit by the fire—me reading a book or stitching old fabric together, her sitting on the nook by the windowsill, looking out to sea and occasionally humming a song, sometimes soft, sometimes mournful—until the fire embers burned out. Then I'd go to sleep in my bed, and her in her warm bath, cocooned in the water. I imagined what that must feel like—to feel safe and warm in something as all-consuming as water. As my world had shrunk, her world had grown. I began to wonder if there were others like her. How had she come to be?

After a week together, the storms had fully settled, bringing blue skies and warmth, and she was strong enough to return to the beach. I felt a pang as we walked down together in a quiet procession, and she paused by the edge of the water. With a glance back at me with her wide black eyes, and toothy smile, she walked forwards until the sea rose up to her midriff. Then, she turned and put out a webbed hand, her other thumbing the bracelet I'd made her on her wrist. She made a noise in the wind, and all I could hear was a murmur.

*Come. Join me.*

But even as I tried, even as I wanted to walk forwards into the blue, I couldn't bring myself to join her.

'Stay,' I said, the word feeling weak even as I said it.

She tilted her head, then stepped forward out of the water, and for a moment I thought she might stay. That she might not leave me. But she just reached out a hand to me. Touched the hag stone I had looped around my neck for a moment, before moving her fingers up my throat, gently, resting on the place where her gills would have been. Then, she leaned into me in an embrace, and I let myself be enveloped by her. Her soft seaweed-hair wrapped around me with its saltsweet smell, while her skin was cool and smooth.

Then, she made a noise in the back of her throat, covered her gills on her neck with her hands, and tried again. '*Stay*,' she said in a distorted voice, and my heart leapt just for a moment until she added. '*No.*'

When the sea witch, turned away and disappeared into the sea this time, I felt a tightness in my throat. I cried until the moon rose into the sky, then I shivered in the coldness of the night.

~

The sea witch didn't return to the beach. Even as I waited and watched the water from the distance, making my little piles of debris that were so small by now, and hoped to see her movement in the corner of my eye once more.

I was alone again. I sat every day in our spot until sunset. I held my bracelet and thought of her, touched my neck absently where she'd touched it, now dry with an itch I could never seem to scratch.

Then, one night, as I prepared to leave the beach and return to the cottage, the hag stone she'd left me that I'd wove so carefully slipped off from round my neck. It clattered to the pebbles below in a sound like a whisper. When I picked it up again, I found myself looking through the hole to the sea. There was a splash in the distance, a ripple on the water. I walked closer for a better look, stone held to my eye all the time. I could hear the closeness of the water. Closer than I'd been in years. And then my toes dipped in the shallow waves, and I didn't recoil from it. The water's touch prickled my skin, cold and warm at the same time, reminding me of her. The sound of the sea was like a song, beckoning me forwards, and I heard her words again carried on the wind.

*Come. Join me.*

I tried to call out to her to come back, but no words came out, only a strangled cry. It was like I'd forgotten how to speak. I fastened the stone pendant around my neck again and as my fingers touched my throat I felt the dry ridges along it, fluttering softly with my breath. In the distant grey sea, a head bobbed above the water, dark hair and black eyes, round and reflecting the fullness of the moon.

I'd not been in the sea for a long time. Could barely remember how to swim. But as I waded into the water to take the outstretched hand of the sea witch, swam with her down and down into the darkness, I remembered not only how to swim, but how to breathe again.

# The Constellations of Daughter Death

When Death decided he wanted a child, he plucked a ghost orchid from the furthest edge of the world—the kind of flower that could survive in the dark indeterminate edges between life and death—and grew her from its roots.

Born from blackened soil, Daughter Death was a quiet baby. She simply gazed upwards and watched the sky, the roots of the above-world trailing through the whorl of obsidian clouds. Her eyes were round and silver like the coins gifted for the dead, and her smile was a crescent-moon, a sliver peeking light into the darkness. When she looked upon her father and reached out with chubby little hands to grab the skeletal ridges of his face, Death was immediately besotted.

Daughter Death became his pride and joy, a girl grown from such dark places that she could bloom anywhere. Everywhere she crawled, moths chased her luminescence, fluttering between her shoulders, settling within her hair, so that soon she was adorned with a cocoon crown. Occasionally moths would hatch and fly free, in search of gaps to break into the brighter world above. In these moments, Death would find himself worrying whether his Daughter's own luminescence could last in his world.

Did any part of her know what lay above? In her dreams, did she imagine visiting the place where mothwings fluttered at dusk, and plants stretched towards the sun, not through the earth?

Between his travels, above and between, Death watched his daughter carefully, her expressions the shape of commas and question marks as she narrowed her glow-in-the-dark eyes and pointed to the sky and kept reaching.

It was the strangest thing, but she one day reached far enough into the above-world, that she was able to pluck something from it. A daisy, which she planted at her feet. At first, the flower remained closed, petals folded over in eternal night. Frustrated, Daughter Death tried to uncurl the petals gently, but they'd always retreat after she let go. She cried for the first time, then, tears silver like comet-trails across her cheeks.

On his next visit to the above-world, Death plucked more daisies from a field to bring home. But when he returned, the flowers were ash in his hands. Daughter Death still took the gift and sprinkled the remains around her own daisy, life and death, together.

~

Daughter Death kept searching for a way to make the flower bloom. She reached as far as she could, past the tallest mountains, through the brightest aurora, into the space above both worlds. There, Daughter Death plucked a star, like her surrounded by darkness, and planted it beside the daisy. The flower awoke and blossomed, casting the space around her aglow. Though Death found it strange, the look in his daughter's eyes consoled him—shining so bright as if galaxies themselves lay within.

~

As Daughter Death's meadow grew, she crafted daisy chains imbued with starlight, gifting one to Death himself. So, Death came to be adorned with her symbol of light, so that everywhere he went, he was reminded of how she bloomed and glowed. Even those he sought in the above-world found themselves drawn to the daisies with a smile, before willingly, accepting his hand.

~

As Daughter Death's imagination grew, so did her power. Once, she captured a fly from the air, the kind that used to float aimlessly in the between-skies of the living and dead. As she held it in her palm, mouth scrunched up into an eclipse, the fly began glowing with a light so bright that when she let it go, it danced fireworks in the dark. One by one, she captured and released her newest creations into the land above, becoming little torches for wanderers on darkened nights.

Then came other luminescence where dark usually swallowed parts of the above-world whole. Daughter Death travelled the length and breadth of the land of death, so she could reach through the watery abysses of the above-sky, where oceans broke upon grey shores. Her hands grabbed jellyfish and algae, and odd-looking fish lurking in the darkest of depths, and lit them blue with phosphorescence.

Later, she journeyed far to the darkest corners of the below-world, pushed hands up through thick black peat to the above-fens and bogs. There, she set gases alight to dance amidst the fog and reeds, and come to be known as spirit lights, leading travellers to treasure, if they did not in their misfortune find Death.

Next, in spectral trees she wandered, with her cloak of daisies and her cocoon crown, where she reached past the tallest canopies, through gnarled sky-roots, breaking into the above-world woodlands. She found mushrooms, touched their mycelium hearts, and set them thrumming with a glow that dappled forest floors, atop rotted wood, between layers of lichen, beside carpets of moss, casting pinpricks of brightness under the cold night sky.

Soon these new lights spilled through into the land of death, the skies now glittering with constellations of Daughter Death's own making. Horizons and canopies speckled with fireflies, fungi, and phosphorescence.

~

Death spent many long nights pondering his daughter's creations. Where he brought darkness and decay, she brought a vibrance. A balance. This land was now as much hers as it was his.

When Death steered people here, Daughter Death would wait to greet them, with her wide silver eyes and thin crescent smile, and her hands that were half in and out of the skies above and below. She'd show them her constellations, and if one light snuffed out, she'd have them close their eyes and make a wish. As they held their breaths, she'd reach out to ignite something new in the above-world so that when they opened their eyes again, they witnessed a new light flash in the dark. It was a promise, from Daughter Death herself. That there was nothing to fear, no darkness she couldn't overcome. And that here, in the land of death, a long, luminous life awaited.

# A Kelpie's Breath

Ada took a deep breath and blew her wish out to sea. Her mother had once told her that the sea could grant a wish—though it would come with a sacrifice. That part had always scared her but now was a time of dire need. Whatever sacrifice she must make, she was ready—for the sake of her home and family. Her wish was to bring the sun and warmth back to the island, so that the crops would grow again, and the sea would settle. She knew it was a lot to ask.

Every morning following, Ada stood on the shore, feet sinking into sand, cold ebbing into her frail bones, waiting for winter to end and for her wish to be granted. As solstice approached, the waves grew more violent than usual, and Ada was about to give up and return home. But then a sliver of sunlight broke through the clouds and lit up a patch of sea as if it was on fire. Striding into the brightness, the form of a creature was unmistakable. A mane as thick as cotton wool but moving like silk in the breeze, trailing seaweed behind like broken and rusted chains.

The creature stepped towards her. Her heart raced. Something stirred in her mind, a story from long ago that said that Kelpies come and go with the tides, taking offerings to the waves. Was this the sea's way of granting her wish?

'I have nothing to offer except my gratitude,' she told the Kelpie, but her words were swallowed by the growing wind.

The Kelpie trod forwards, her hooves barely making an imprint in the soft sand. She whinnied and tossed her head back, revealing a bridle of polished silver. Water drip-dripped from her mane, darkening the sand in her wake. Closer and closer she came, until Ada could smell her breath—sweet like juniper berries, but smoky like peat. The Kelpie bowed her head, knelt with one leg forwards, and looked at Ada with sad, sea-glass eyes. Then Ada understood.

She glanced back at her island home. So much of it was different from how it had been in her youth—no longer did the flowers blossom, no longer did seabirds cry overhead, no longer could boats leave the harbour no matter the season. Maybe now it could return to the way it had been, for her children and grandchildren. She closed her eyes and sucked in salty air through her teeth, feeling the sting in her cheeks for one last time.

'Will it hurt?' she asked.

The Kelpie brayed, her breath forming a mist between them, spindly wisps reaching out. Ada found her fingers intertwining with the mane, and she pulled herself up, settling in the withers. The Kelpie took one final look at Ada's island and strode into the sea, until together they melted into the froth and foam of passing waves.

As the sea stilled, the clouds parted. Blue broke grey. Light shone on glittering sand. When the first islander awoke, a piercing cry from a skua rang overhead. In spindly wild grasses, a dandelion bloomed.

# The Wulver's Gift

The first pie appeared on the windowsill on a summer morning, during a season where the sun had been so hot it had withered the soil and parched the rivers dry. It had been a season of scarcity, yet here on the window, a fresh fish pie, steaming hot and smelling of herbs and butter. Fi and her family gathered round it, wondering what neighbour had left such a treat. She took it inside where it sat untouched on the table and pushed her children's grabbing hands away.

Outside, in the square, a chattering crowd gathered. Fi joined them, noticing some holding dishes looking lost, as if wondering who to return them to. Her neighbour Oonagh had received a winterberry pie, while Andrew from across the square had an apple one.

'Witchcraft!' Morag, one of the town's elders, said to the crowd. 'No one touch them. They're cursed.'

'It's a test of our resolve,' the Priest said, joining the fray. 'We must resist temptation.'

But others weren't convinced. 'No reason to let good food go to waste,' Oonagh said, holding her own pie to her chest.

'Maybe it's a gift from the gods,' Andrew suggested to the sceptical Priest.

Fi thought of her hungry children and the decadent-smelling meal at home. She listened distantly as the townsfolk argued, and then as the town split, some of them discarding their dishes, the others taking them, Fi returned home.

She smelt the pie first for any sign of obvious poison, then took burning sage and wafted it over the top to throw off any curses. Then she dug in. It was creamy and delicious, and after an hour or so of no harmful effects, she heated it up. The family ate well that night.

~

The gifts continued, pies in all shapes and varieties, savoury and sweet, appearing overnight on windowsills. And so the rift in the town grew: the ones who ate and the ones who didn't, the latter getting more and more irate as they watched their full-bellied neighbours chatter about their latest feast.

There were continued murmurings of witchcraft, devilry and trickster gods, and a night patrol was set up to catch whatever was leaving the gifts, circling the houses by cover of night. For days the suspect eluded them. Whatever skulked leaving food and gifts stayed in the shadows, out of sight.

Most townsfolk when they did such acts of goodwill did so with the prospect of acclaim. But this stranger did everything without expectation of reward. Whoever they were, Fi was grateful. So, one evening, she left her own gift on the windowsill. A charm pendant woven from old fishing rope and a polished stone from the river. The next morning, the pendant was gone, and a thick loaf of bread with honey and jam was in its place.

~

The first sighting came some days later. Morag had stayed up all night, watching by her window, waiting. And there, she said, prowled a creature so foul she almost passed out from the sight. A monster with the head of a wolf and the body of a man. She called a town meeting to hunt it down.

But Fi countered with her own meeting—with Oonagh, Andrew and the others who'd accepted the gifts.

'We have to find the wolf before they do,' Fi said.

'You don't think he really is trying to curse us?' Andrew asked.

'What would he have to gain?' Fi said. 'We should wait together, then follow his trail. Tonight, before the others can decide on what evil to concoct.'

And so Fi, her family, and the group of townsfolk waited all together hidden with a view of Fi's windowsill. As they saw the wolf man swap a gift Fi had left for a new tray of goods, they skulked through the shadows themselves and followed him. He led them along bogs and moors, down the riverbank and towards the sea. As the sun rose, the land opened to a small homestead on a peninsula. Bees buzzed from hives surrounded by wildflower meadows. Goats bleated and cows lowed in green pastures. And there was the wolf man, approaching his creatures with a bucket.

On his shoulder was a fishing rod, and a satchel with herbs sticking out.

When he saw them approach, the wolf man hid behind his animals, paws held out. 'Please.' His voice was a growl. 'I mean no harm.'

'No need to worry about us.' Fi smiled at him, noticing he was wearing the stone pendant. 'How can we help?'

The man lowered his paws and nodded, welcoming them. And so the townsfolk helped the man tend his land of plenty. As the afternoon wore on, he told them about his animals, the bees, the soil, the hedgerows and trees, and the wildlife that thrived between. They started to learn what they could for their own town, so that when the next dry season hit, they'd be better prepared.

As the sky reddened, Morag and her group of naysayers arrived in a rabble, pouring towards the peninsula like chattering geese. Fi stood her ground by the wolf man, her own group outnumbering the others. Morag's nose scrunched up at the sight, eyes flashing between them and the wolf.

'There's no witch hunt for you here, Morag,' Fi said.

The wolf man stepped out to greet them. In his hands, he held out a basket of vegetables and a bucket of fresh milk. Though Morag flinched, especially as Fi's children peered around his legs with faces covered in giggles and berries, the other townsfolk softened and saw only kindness. One by one, they left Morag's group and joined the others.

Later, as Morag skulked around the homestead watching the others get to work, Fi saw her sneak to the windowsill and pick up an oatcake with a slice of cheese. The old woman ate it with a flash of a toothy smile.

# Seedseeker

Ever since her first dive, Ailish knew she wanted to be a Seedseeker. Standing now on the deck under the wind-sail, ready for the dive that will decide her future, her stomach twists like a tangle of seaweed. The crew of the Gaia look on, even the ship's cat, Marsden whose narrow yellow eyes are trained on her and the rest of the new recruits.

Beside her, Ollie—her best friend, and biggest rival—is grinning stupidly and he nudges her shoulder as they step forwards. But she ignores him. He wants to be a Seedseeker too, and there's only space for one more on this ship. The others are less of a worry, at least—Runa wants to be a cartographer, and Sammy a fisher. It's only Ollie that could steal away her future.

The Captain steps forwards and hits the ceremonial bell. It's time. Ailish approaches, body tensed, and the Captain hands her the weighted belt with a nod. Ailish nods back but tries not catch her gaze. Tries not to betray her nerves. She ties the belt around her waist and fits the goggles and breathing gear until her breaths echo in her ears. Then with a final look at Ollie who gives her another smile and a thumbs-up, which she doesn't return, she kisses her fingers and salutes the sky for luck, before jumping into the water below.

The cold sting of the sea wraps around her, though to her it's a warm embrace. It always has been. It feels like going home. The water is clearer than usual—there's not been a storm for a few days—so she can just about see the seabed. Glittering sediment catches the sun here and there like tiny pieces of treasure. Bubbles rise as she kicks downwards, and in the corner of her eye she sees Ollie dive down to the right. She doesn't follow him though, and instead veers to the left.

Soon, towers of buildings rise to her side in strange reefs, and she counts the buildings as she passes in a sequence she's imprinted to memory. The town is like a ghost, faded rows of concrete swallowed whole by the rising sea, a grey snapshot of the world before. Yet, it's beautiful in its way, and will always remind her of the fragility of things. Still, life continues to beat within the cracks. Kelp clings in holdfasts to jutting rocks, while fish swim in and out of broken windows or rotting doors. She never could imagine living in a permanent home like that. The Gaia is all she's ever known beyond the floating islands they sometimes visit on trading stops.

Growing up, she and Ollie dove and explored these long-gone towns, looking for hidden treasures. Her cabin on the Gaia is filled with items from the world before, memories her descendants left behind: sun-dried pages from water-logged books that she sticks to her wall to try and fill in the gaps of the stories within, chipped porcelain cups with bright designs that she uses for planting herbs and flowers, plastic toys and broken electronics, and a wooden cat statue that looks just like Marsden. He likes to come into her room sometimes just to stare at it with an inquisitive look for a while before curling up at the end of her bed.

For now, she passes the towering buildings without stopping to search for trinkets. After counting the eighth row, she traverses a side street, kicks out against the current for a few more minutes, then breaks into the open sea again. In the distance, the seagrass meadow looms like a field of emeralds dazzling in the sun, and her body bubbles with excitement and adrenaline.

When she and Ollie first visited this meadow, they had sunk down into it. They lay in the seagrass together until their oxygen supply ran out, watching as the sun cast silhouettes on the dappled water above. When fish swam by, they traced shapes in the water with bubbles, and the curious creatures followed the pattern as if dancing. After that dive, she and Ollie sat on the crow's nest together watching the stars above, wrapped up warm in seagrass-woven blankets, and drinking hand-cut kelp soup. When a shooting star passed above, Ollie told her to close her eyes and make a wish, and she wished then and there that she could be a Seedseeker. Since then it had been all she'd ever wanted. Ollie never told her what he wished for. But when she opened her eyes, he was already looking over her with his wide smile, the moon reflecting a dash of silver in his green-eyed gaze. Then he took her hand and placed something cold in her palm. Ailish looked down and thumbed the grey stone, round and smooth, with a hole in its centre.

'What's this for?' she asked, frowning.

'It's a magic stone. I found it in the seagrass beds today.'

'It's beautiful.' She made to hand it back to him, but he shook his head. 'It's for you. A gift.'

She smiled. 'What did I do to deserve a friend like you?'

He didn't reply straight away, he just kept looking at her with an odd expression, almost like Marsden when he was looking at the cat statue. Then Ollie guided her hand gently upwards so that the hole in the stone faced the night sky above. 'If you look through it, to the stars, it will help you see into the otherworld,' he explained.

Ailish nodded slowly. 'I hope it helps my wish come true.'

'Mine too,' he replied as she clutched the stone.

'Thank you,' she whispered, and she leaned into his shoulder, feeling the beat of his heart in rhythm with the waves sloshing below. She stayed there with Ollie all night until the sun rose red with the dawn, thinking of magic, strange worlds beyond the stars, and what her future might look like.

Now she's searching for that answer. All she needs is a single seed, and her destiny will be secured. Her job will be, forever more, a Seedseeker. She will spend her days diving into the blue, searching for seagrass seeds, then replanting them in meadows new and old, so that when she returns as the ship does its yearly rounds, the meadows will grow and grow. Though she wasn't alive for what happened before, the Gaia is working to undo some of the damage of the past, and so this job feels like a purpose she was born for. Now, as she swims forwards she can feel the hug of the sea around her, urging her on, welcoming her to this underwater world with open arms.

At the seagrass meadow, she slows to scan the area. The first thing she picks up will determine her fate. She dives closer to the seabed, searching for the perfect spot. When she reaches the older plants growing together in thick clumps, she stops, and is about to dig into the sand when something else catches her eye—a round stone with a hole bored in the middle. Just like the one Ollie got her. She reaches for it. Holds the smooth coldness in her palm. And just like that, her fate is decided. Her heart sinks as she realises her error. Now the weight of water pushing down on her feels less like an embrace but a curse. She doesn't want to swim back up anymore, to face her crew, to be assigned her fate. The thought crosses her mind that she could leave the stone, find a seed instead, and no one would ever know. But *she* would know. This stone was the first thing she touched, and that is the rule they live by. Even if she lied, she knows that in time the guilt would swallow her whole, just like the sea swallowed the sunken cities. She looks up, her breath hitching in her throat as panic rises. But there's nothing else to do but swim home and face her Captain, Ollie, the rest of the crew and her future.

She rises to the surface with a loud puff of air and the sounds of clapping and cheers follow. She doesn't feel like celebrating. She scans the Gaia—first back. Dejected and cold, she climbs up to the deck. When Marsden curls his body around her ankle in greeting, she pushes him away, but it just makes her guilt grow as he sits just beyond her reach, scowling in silent judgement.

One by one, the others arrive. Ollie's hand is closed over a clump of sand. Runa has an old brass compass and brandishes it with a wide smile. Then there's Sammy with a small fish magnet that catches the sun and reflects a rainbow prism of light on the Gaia's deck. All of them are out of breath, but none look unhappy. Ollie waves at her, trying to catch her eye, but she keeps clutching her stone to her chest and looks to the sky, avoiding his gaze, avoiding looking at what else lies in the clump of sand in his hand.

The Captain calls Ailish forwards first, and head bowed she approaches and holds out her hand.

'A seer stone,' the Captain says after a moment. 'A rare find.'

Ailish looks up. 'What does it mean?'

'Why do you look so worried?'

Ailish chews her salt-dry lips, then she looks to Ollie who's still grinning. Between his fingers, a tiny thread of seagrass glistens. She sighs. 'I wanted to be a Seedseeker, but now that's Ollie, and there's no place for me.'

The Captain laughs softly and puts a hand on Ailish's shoulder. Then, from her pocket, she takes out a piece of dried seagrass-thread and loops it into the stone to make a necklace. 'You two have always done everything together, as one, so why would we change that now?' She ties the stone so that it rests above Ailish's heart. 'To keep you both safe, Seedseekers.'

Ailish looks around at her crew. Ollie cocks his head with a telling look as if he knew this was how it would always end. That no matter what, they'd stay together. As if he wished it long ago, and now it was so.

'Wait,' she says looking at him, and she takes the necklace off. From her pocket she takes out the seer stone that Ollie gave to her years before, that she's always kept in her pocket, to remind her of wishes, otherworlds, and destiny. And, she understands now, to remind her of him. She swaps the stones out, then loops some thread around the new one. She holds it in the air first and looks through it towards Ollie on the other side, realising that maybe destiny and magic has many shapes. She steps up to Ollie and he leans in as she lifts it over his neck.

'To keep you safe, Seedseeker,' she repeats the Captain's words And for a long moment he just looks at her with that stupid smile of his, his freckles like constellations on his cheeks, his eyes as green as the meadows beneath the sea. Then, he's leaning forwards, his hands on her arms, and she kisses him. His lips taste of salt and sea, and she drinks in the feeling, the same feeling of the sea's warm embrace. And she's never been surer of her choice than in this moment. After, she loops her arm around Ollie's, and she turns rosy-cheeked to the now smiling crew.

'About time,' the Captain says, and the others laugh. As the Captain continues the ceremony with Runa and Sammy, Marsden curls around their ankles, and Ailish looks to Ollie who just shrugs and pulls her in closer.

Their fate assigned, together the crew of the Gaia hold their talismans as they look out to sea and salute to the horizon. Tomorrow, her future begins, but tonight, they celebrate.

# The Last Call
of the Deep

*They say her teeth are carved from fallen stars, strong like diamonds.*
*They say her skin is formed of the sun, glittering silver and gold.*
*They say her eyes are powered by the moon, jewelled beacons in the deep.*
*They say she has lived for thousands of years.*
*They say she's the last of her kind.*

~

*The waves crest and fall as she travels endlessly in the deep. Existing through the generations, she calls out to relatives and friends. Back and forth as the currents guide, she gathers stories from continents and cultures, and they latch in her mind like the barnacles on her skin. Tides welcome each movement of her body, while seafarers quake at her voice. A low, mournful echo that can be heard by her own kind hundreds of miles away.*

*But lately, when she calls, there's been no reply. Her voice drifts alone, stretching into the gulf as if swallowed by a black hole. She has become the keeper of stories, with no one to share them with.*

~

It's almost too dark to see when she breaches the water with a puff of air and a smooth undulation of her curves. She gazes up with a moonlit eye, searching for an island she knows was once here. Though her vision is hazy, she can see there's little rising above the water—just a small hillock, barren and desolate.

She tries to remember the last time she travelled in these parts, but time spent in the deep passes differently, so that days and weeks and years seem almost to merge together.

Still, something isn't as it was.

Diving a little below the surface, she swims forwards to investigate, sending out a call, listening to how the echo reverberates back to her. It tells her that a vast obstacle lies ahead, under the water. With eyes adjusting to the murk, she spins on her side and looks at the strange world now surrounding her—mountains and rows of tiny derelict trees line one part, while valleys ebb in steady waves on the other. Amidst the landscape lie buildings of mortar and stone, now uninhabited. Seaweed and shells cling to the sides of walls, while tiny fish bubble back and forth from the maw-like windows.

She calls out again, pushing her voice beyond the underwater fortress, crying. *Have I lost my way?*

She swims past the ruins and waits with faltering hope for a response. None comes. It's been so long since she heard another voice in the deep. So long since she's come across another of her kin. So long since she's collected a story from afar.

She thinks of her last calf from many cycles ago. He was a curious one, enjoying swimming up to floating wooden islands, saying hello to seafarers who had for a time greeted them like long lost friends. But one afternoon, when he was almost grown, she'd let him go to see one of them on his own. He didn't return. When she swam out to look for him, the only evidence of his presence was an oily residue in the water, slick and metallic to the taste. She cried then, a deep siren call, as she knew the floating island had taken him.

It wasn't long after that incident, that she stopped meeting or hearing her kind at all—as if they had all vanished along with her son.

Struggling to make sense of her swirling thoughts, she swims on, intent on heading north, following cooling waters as the seasons change—as she has done for as long as she can remember. Maybe things will become clearer there.

~

The sunken island isn't the first of its kind that she finds. Drowned worlds lie beneath the surface where once she knew there were coastlines and vast swathes of land. It disorients her, this peculiar new tiding, and she finds she can no longer tell where in her journey she is. Will she ever reach north, or will she end up circling endlessly, searching for something that may no longer exist?

She calls out again, but there's still silence.

~

She loses track of how long she's been swimming for. She stops for the occasional meal, but supplies in these waters have become harder to find. At this time of year, there ought to be a bounty of life. Her energy begins to wane.

The seas eventually start to cool, and it eases some of her tension. She feels a shift in her body as the water whirls around her. When she was young, her family would tell a story that her ancestors formed the continents—that the great creatures before once breached the surface and simply fell asleep, body half out of the water, the rest of them rooted to the ocean below. Where they lay, land gathered, forming rocks and mountains and rolling hills. They became the world that once was.

It made sense, in a way—an endless sleep, to begin a cycle anew. Is this to be her fate?

Perhaps it's time to let go, to become like her ancestors.

She lets out a long breath and allows her body to drift to the surface. There she stretches out, until she's lying with her underside facing the brightness of the sun. The rays feel warm on her skin. It's peaceful here. And suddenly all she wants to do is sleep.

As she closes her eyes, every story she's ever heard flashes through her mind, until all she can think of is the water around her and the sun on her skin, as if she's letting the tales go into the depths beneath her. She hopes that the story of her ancestors is true—that her body will merge with the sea somehow, that she will become something more than herself.

It's a calming drift into a long slumber, and she's vaguely aware of the nights turning to day and the days to night, as stars and the sun and the moon flash by above.

When it is time, she uses her final breath to send out a sombre call.

Her heartbeat slows. Her body stiffens, turning to rock and stone.

~

*They say her call was formed of melancholy and hope.*
*They say it was the last call of the deep.*
*But as time moves on and the tides come and go, something new awakens.*
*Far away, in distant waters, a call echoes back.*

# DAUGHTER OF FIRE AND WATER

## A NOVELLA

*May Brida, daughter of Callie, of fire and water, be banished to the under-realm, contained by her flesh and skin, so that she may only pass from the mountain at the turn of the season, when her power may bless the world anew.*

# PART ONE

The mortal arrived in our under-realm at the end of a long winter. Just as the storms had settled leaving surging rivers in their wake, the sailor had taken the treacherous route from the coast to the mountain where my mother Callie—ruler of all deities and the realms—had cruelly imprisoned me for a mistake I'd made long ago. I wonder now if he had any expectations as to what he would find when he got here, if he knew that he would find so much more than an adventure fit for a future king. But such is the folly of mortals—they do not know the limits of their desire. A deity's folly is more dangerous however, and that is mostly what this story is about. That, and love, freedom, and retribution. But not necessarily in that order.

It was cold and peaceful in the cavern at the heart of the mountain as the long winter night set in. I was sitting on a bench beside the small viewpoint at the cavern's furthest corner, weaving a blanket and enjoying the slight flow of air that ebbed through the cracks. I called it a viewpoint, though it was really just a gap in the rocks, but it was the only place apart from the mountain's peak that offered a view of the outside world, however slight. The only other light came from the hearths that I was forced to keep burning in each corner, casting strange shadows across the stone columns and high ceilings.

There was a loud sigh, and I cast an eye over to the centre of the cavern where my brother Cernun was lazing cross-legged by Callie's ancient spring, gazing down at the dark surface as though expecting it to show him his future. He knew as well as me that the water from the spring was only used at the turn of the seasons and that nothing from within the under-realm itself could touch its surface. Still, I found it a useful conduit for my Sight when I needed it, and the slowly bubbling water at least had a calming effect.

My brother, on the other hand, did not. He was hunched over on the quartz steps, his head tilted so that his copper-tinged antlers caught the flicker of light from one of the fires behind. It pained me to see him like this—not because I pitied him, but because I didn't understand how he was content with wasting his time inside when he could have been outside roaming and exploring in the wilderness and fresh air. During winter, I was at my most restless. The growing cold marked the longest period between my freedom and entrapment, with the knowledge of the long months of darkness and boredom ahead. I'd have given anything to be in Cernun's position, to have even a few days of his freedom, yet he didn't seem to care. If he was only allowed three short days a year outside the mountain, he'd understand—but he only thought about his own torment and curse, never mine. Gods are rather self-involved, after all.

Cernun began to spin his shield beside him like it was a toy, the grating noise setting my teeth on edge. I put my weaving down and walked over to him. 'Why must you sit like that?' I perched beside him on the steps that led down to the water.

He glanced up at me with contempt. 'Like what?' As if he knew it would annoy me, he spun his shield again so that it sliced against the stone with a screech.

I winced. 'In that stupid position. You look ridiculous, Cernun. And stop playing with your shield, the sound is giving me a headache. Some of us are trying to do something useful with our time in this cursed place.'

He ignored me and spun the shield again. 'How would you like me to sit, dear sister?'

'Preferably not here at all,' I said. 'I'll never understand how you choose to stay in this prison when you could be out there.' I glanced towards a far corridor that led to a spiral staircase and the waterfall pool at the base of the mountain: where freedom beckoned Cernun, and taunted me.

'Have you seen the weather?' he said. 'It's cold and miserable.'

'Anywhere is better than being stuck here.'

He raised an eyebrow. 'You overestimate the appeal. Always greener, so to speak.'

'In this case, that is exactly true. All that's here is desolation.'

'Well, desolation suits me,' he said with a huff of breath.

I looked him up and down. 'I can see that. But if you don't want to go outside, I would happily take your place.'

He looked me dead in the eye. 'Must we do this again?'

I lowered my voice a little. 'Let me inhabit your mind again, just for a day. It's been too long since I've used my Sight with you, brother.'

His mouth curved ever so slightly. 'You really must contain your desperation. Besides, it is far too much for me to risk without reward, especially after what happened last time…'

I rolled my eyes. Of course he'd bring that up—the time I'd inhabited his body, and we'd travelled too far only to be spotted by mortals on a hunting trip. Seeing him in his half-human form, they'd tried to kill him, and with me inside his head Cernun was slow to react. Though we just got away, it was far too close for comfort. For a while after, mortals stalked the land near our under-realm until our mother sent an avalanche to get rid of them. Now my brother brought it up whenever I upset him, threatening to tell Callie it was all my fault so that she might find a way to take even my Sight away. 'We'll be more careful this time,' I pushed on despite my own worries. 'I don't even need to go far. We'll stay away from mortals.'

'Wouldn't you rather wait until Spring?'

I shook my head. 'I haven't felt properly cold in years.'

'Lucky you. I wish you'd turn the temperature up in here, the fires are barely embers.'

I glanced at one of the hearths in the corner, with its feeble orange glow. For years, I had been reducing the fires gradually, each time only by a fraction so our mother didn't notice. I hoped it would be part of my way out of this place, conserving my power until I found a means to escape. But my brother—watching and sulking in the under-realm almost as much as I did—noticed the change. I knew he wouldn't tell her, even if he would hold it over me on occasion. 'I have to conserve my energy for more important things.'

He tutted. 'Like inhabiting your brother's mind?'

'That's different.'

'If you say so.' He paused, then skulked towards me, head bowed into the shadows so that his eye sockets appeared empty. 'We could make a deal, however…'

'No. Forget it.'

His face twisted. 'I'm going to freeze my antlers off. If you turn the heat up, just a little, you can name the day, and I'll willingly go–'

'No,' I repeated, a little more forcefully. 'I'm saving my power.'

'So be it,' he said in a low voice, his expression hardening. 'But don't come crying to me when you've had your short bout of freedom and want another excursion into the cold.'

'Then I'll just have to make it colder in here.'

His jaw clenched. 'You have too much power.'

'You have too much freedom.'

'You don't understand my torment.'

I paused. 'You don't understand mine.'

With that, Cernun lost his temper and hurled his shield across the room. It ricocheted off a column and span towards the pool. As it struck the surface of the water, it bounced off with a loud ringing sound that echoed around the cavernous space. It crashed out and hit my brother square in the stomach. He bent over and yelled out, more in anger than pain.

I lifted my chin and tutted. 'Cernun, you really must contain your desperation.'

My brother roared again and picked up his shield before marching from the room, his footsteps echoing down the dark and lonely corridor. When he was gone, I approached one of the hearths and took a deep breath, summoning my power. As I let out the breath slowly, I pulled in the power of the embers, watching as they dulled.

I knew it was spiteful, but Cernun frustrated me. While he was maybe the only one that understood some of my pain, his torment was, in my estimation, far more deserved—for when he had the freedom to walk this earth year-round, he had switched between man and beast so often that he had become a blend of them both. Yet still he spent much of his time with mortals, many that came to worship, love and fear him, honouring him with unnatural rituals and throwing themselves at him with their own wild desire. Many of his offspring lived unchecked across the land—some with unlearned powers, others with strange animalistic tendencies. Mother eventually had to restrict his access. Although, unlike my three days in spring, he had a six-month window of freedom, wandering in winter and darkness if he wished. The curse was that he despised the cold so much that he barely ventured outside anymore. Callie was clever and cruel in equal measure.

Still, I was envious of Cernun. Surely, I had long served out my own punishment? I deserved more time in the wilderness and the freedom to live how I pleased. Surely I had paid for my mistakes of the past in more ways than one. Callie only wanted to imprison me because I could threaten her rule. But power can be dangerous, especially when forcibly contained.

~

Winter dragged on and on, and I spent much of the daylight looking out from the viewpoint hoping to see early signs of spring. Now that the storms had died down, I began to notice a change in the land. The weather had been more severe than normal for the season. Callie had proclaimed it was the fault of the mortals, who were doing their utmost to squander her efforts, so her attention was being stretched and she had been unable to keep her usual seasonal control. The torrent of freezing sleet and rain burst the boundaries of rivers so that the waterfall now led to a rushing river which stretched as far as I could see into the horizon.

As I watched a bird dip and dive over the water, I spotted something come round a far bend. It moved against the current, the wind pushing it closer hour by hour until I could just make out its shape. A sailboat. Which meant... *a mortal? Here?*

My heart began to race—no mortal had come near us in years, not since my mother had cursed me at least. Had an adventurer come to seek the will of the gods? What stories had they heard about our fortress home? Or maybe we were simply a matter of myth and legend by now, and this sailor was only exploring the new route created by the expanded river.

The boat twisted towards the base of the mountain and finally arrived at the waterfall pool. I shivered, looking behind me to check if Cernun or my mother had seen the boat too. Callie would cast any mortals away or send a wave to drown them—she held an unrivalled bitterness towards them. She said they could not understand the ways of the land, that they abused their freedoms only to pillage and plunder and fight over resources. And so, safe upon her mountain throne above us, she would send them storms, hardship, a way to balance the power between man and beast and beast and landscape. I thought that it must get tiring to cast judgement from afar, but Callie showed no desire to be among mortals and so had no understanding as to why I desired to be. It was a different, blissful, existence when I had such freedom before.

She took all of that away from me.

I had to get closer—to meet whoever was on the boat, to see why they had come, to experience something that wasn't just this cold and dark isolation. Maybe I could even speak to them, get news from afar.

Quietly, I crossed the cavern and headed towards the spiral staircase. The air grew more and more stale the further I descended, like death lay within the granite walls around me. My legs felt tense. I hadn't been down to the lowest cave in a while. The waterfall always felt too close to freedom. I could stand behind the water, watching the lands beyond, but I was unable to step into daylight.

As I finally reached the bottom, there was a sharp chill in the air, and the freshness of it was a welcome reprieve. The fire had almost gone in the cave, so I closed my eyes and summoned the slightest of embers to light my way.

The warmth of the act felt strange on my skin, prickling with hairs and goosebumps rising. I crept across uneven rocks to peer through the slight gap between the crashing waterfall and the cave wall, hoping to get a better look at our visitor. A mortal was standing on the deck of the boat. He turned and looked straight towards where I stood. I inhaled sharply and stepped back. Had he noticed the fire? Had he seen me? What if he came close? Would I be able to talk to him? I couldn't help but think of the last time I'd been in the company of a mortal—when getting tied up in their affairs had led only to pain. As I pondered whether it would be better to leave the cavern and the man alone, I peered out again, unable to quell my curiosity.

Our eyes met. His were a striking green, vibrant like the grass in spring, a stark contrast to his hair which was dark and rugged like the soil of the earth. His broad body was wrapped in layers of fur and leather, so that he looked almost like a bear. More like a god than a mortal. Though the way he held himself was more diminished, like he was uncertain how to stand in his own body. He dug an oar into the water and the boat drifted closer to the waterfall entrance.

'Hello?' his voice echoed into the space, almost drowned out by the sound of the thrashing water. 'Come, let me see you better.'

It was strangely comforting to hear a mortal voice, a young one without the bitter twang that marked the tone of my mother and brother. His accent was soft, lilting. Noble, even. My heart in my throat, I crept forward a little, allowing myself to be visible in the gap between the rocks and water.

His face lit up at the sight of me. 'Are you lost, fair maiden?'

I frowned. 'Do not call me fair maiden.'

'I am sorry,' he said, eyes narrowing. 'What shall I call you?

'Brida,' I replied.

His smile back was broad and friendly, an expression I'd not seen in a long time. 'Well, Brida of the waterfall, are you lost?'

I shook my head. 'I'm not lost.'

'Then come out from under there so that I may look upon you without this wall between us,' he urged. He pushed his oar in again to keep his boat steady, neck craning to see me better.

'I cannot.'

'Why ever not?'

'Because I may not leave this mountain, by my mother's decree.'

'Who is your mother to have imposed such a cruel fate?'

'Callie of the Mountain. You might have heard of her.'

His eyes widened and he looked behind him as though expecting to see her there, gliding towards him on the river. 'Daughter of Callie?' He turned back to me. 'If that is the case, I really must see you better.' With that, he jumped into the water and waded towards the rocks. He clambered up them with grace and strength and made to come under the waterfall.

I held my hand up. 'Wait. This place…it might not be safe for you.'

He paused, but only for a second. 'I am willing to take the risk.'

He stepped forwards into the gap, the water splashing across his shoulders and long flowing hair. Close up he was even more handsome. His jaw strong, his bright eyes round and kind

He beamed at me. 'You must forgive me for calling you fair maiden, for I should have called you a goddess of beauty.'

'You flatter me.'

'I am not sure I could ever find true words to describe you, but until then I will flatter as I can.'

I laughed and stepped further into the cavern, inviting him in. His eyes remained fixed on me, entranced. The last mortal that had looked at me in that way did so after a long time spent together—when we were equals walking the land and there was no one on the Earth I could have felt more comfortable around. I shook the memory away, not wanting to dwell on such painful memories. But maybe this new mortal could truly see me for who I was. 'You are the first mortal I've seen in a long time,' I told him. 'Yet you do not seem like the ones I remember. Perhaps times have changed.'

'Mortal…well, I like to think I am of a different kind than most.' He puffed out his chest a little. 'I am to be a King of our people. And one day I will lead them to a better life full of victory and fortune.'

I sat down, taking care to position myself on a higher rock, signalling to the one beside it. He sat down, continuing to look up at me. The glittering water in his hair reflected the embers of the fire, making it look like he was coated in stardust. 'You have not yet told me your name?'

He smiled. 'Angus. Prince Angus.'

'That is a noble name,' I said. 'Why have you ventured here, Prince Angus?'

'I have heard many stories of this place, so when the rivers rose and carved out the way for us, I had to see for myself.'

I eyed him a little and cocked my head, letting my long auburn hair flow over my shoulder. 'And are you satisfied by what you've found?'

He followed my movements, his eyes hungry. 'I could not be more so.'

It may have been vanity or naivety, but I could not deny that I was enjoying his attention. Here was the first mortal I had seen in what seemed like an age, enamoured by me at first sight. And he was, in his way, a sight to behold. A prince from faraway lands, an adventurer, brave and strong, with high ambitions. Of course I wanted to keep his attentions. 'I am glad you came too. It is an honour to be treated with such company.'

He pushed his shoulders back, the compliment seeming to roll off him. 'It is cruel of your mother to imprison you like this. How has she done it?'

'She cast a curse so that I am bound here, *May Brida, daughter of Callie, of fire and water, be banished to the under-realm, contained by her flesh and skin…*' I sighed. 'I have tried for many years to find a way around it, but I have found none. And only the one who lays a curse may lift it.'

He frowned eyeing me with a curious gaze. 'It is a strange curse indeed. What a shame you cannot shed your skin.'

'What do you mean?'

'Oh.' His expression softened. 'I am only struck that it is a cruel detail that you are entrapped by your flesh and skin, for that is something no one can escape.'

My heart raced and I let out a breath. *Of course…* 'I'm a fool.'

Angus leant back a little, his hand twitching to the axe hilt on his belt, as if expecting me turn into a man-eating reptile at any moment. 'Y-you can't shed your skin…can you?'

'Don't look so afraid, I'm not a snake.'

'Ah, good.' He seemed relieved. 'Though I have heard…interesting tales of the gods and I am not much fond of reptiles.'

I leaned towards him, pointing to his axe. 'Whether I could wield such powers or not, you'd need more than that to kill me.'

His face reddened and he quickly pulled his hand away from the weapon. 'I'm sorry goddess, I meant no insult. An instinct, only,' he said. 'But I still don't understand, why do you say you are a fool?'

I did not answer straight away and instead looked down at my hands. Once, on one of my seasonal excursions I had fallen on some rocks, cutting my hand deeply and breaking a leg. Cernun had been temporarily freed from his imprisonment to find me when I hadn't returned at my sanctioned time. When he took me back, Callie had sped up the healing by dropping a small amount of water from her spring on the wound. Now the skin was smooth, unscarred. No evidence of the injury at all. 'There may be a way,' I told Angus. 'Something I've not thought to try before now. Will you return? I might have a plan, and I think you'll be able to help me.'

Angus looked between me and the stairs which led to the rest of the under-realm. 'Of course. If I can help, it would be my honour to serve a goddess such as you. When should I visit again?'

I thought about it—I knew I'd need to make sure my mother would not see what I was up to. And I'd need to find a way of getting some water from her spring—it would be easier if I waited until dark for that. 'Tomorrow,' I said. 'Meet me at the first light of dawn.'

'I will camp nearby tonight, then,' he said, looking behind him. 'Spring is almost here, it will be warm enough.'

I smiled, looking him up and down once more. 'And I'll need your water flask,' I told him. 'Will you give it to me?'

'Anything, you may have it.' He unclipped it from his belt.

'Thank you.' I held the smoothness of the leather flask in my hands. Nothing from the under-realm could touch Callie's spring, but this could work. Why had I not thought of it before? Maybe this was why Callie had worked so hard to keep mortals away from our mountain. 'When this is done, you will have my full gratitude,' I told him. 'And I will ensure your people are rewarded.'

He shook his head. 'I would do it only because it is the right thing to do.'

'Until tomorrow then,' I said and stood up. 'I must go and make preparations.'

He held his hand out. I gave him mine and he took it, kissed the back of it gently with a low bow. His touch sent a shiver across my skin. It was something I had not felt in a long time. Excitement. Desire. 'I will think of nothing else until you are freed, my Goddess.'

He held my hand for a moment before he let it drop gently and turned to leave. As he returned to his boat, I headed towards the spiral staircase, water flask hidden in my cloak.

*Contained by my flesh and skin.*

I could hardly believe how blind I had been not to have thought of it before. But at least now I had a plan. As I'd have to wait until dark to collect water from the spring, I first headed to my chambers and packed some sparse belongings—a wooden bowl made for me by my former lover, Alder, in the times before my curse, a fine blanket I'd woven to act as a reminder of my years of isolation and why I had chosen to leave, and a selection of dried herbs and tonics I'd gathered and created over the years, in case the water from the spring wasn't quite enough. The thought at what I had to do set a knot in my stomach. But the thrill of what could come after kept me on my path.

I took the pack and hid it behind a rock in the waterfall cave. I then wrote a note to my mother, explaining my leaving, but mostly as a boast of my imminent escape, of how I'd finally found a way to outwit her. All it had taken was a mortal to help me thwart her curse. She'd hate that detail in particular. I placed the note in a lockbox—it didn't have a key, but it was symbolic—and left it on my side table. She'd send her Sight to the under-realm searching for me and find it, but by then I'd be long gone. The idea of her finding me suddenly missing filled me with almost as much excitement as the prospect of leaving.

After dark, when all was still in the under-realm, I snuck from my chambers and padded through winding halls to the central cavern. As I entered, I reduced the fire in the hearths again, pulling as much energy as I could into myself.

I walked towards the spring, half expecting Callie to appear with her blue skin setting the dark room aglow, even though I'd never seen her physically leave her mountain throne. What if she saw my intention with her single eye and struck me down, along with any notion that I might ever be able to escape? Maybe she'd even curse me further, and

I'd find myself confined to my chambers for eternity. I shivered and felt my way to the spring. The water itself moved in soft glimmering waves, blues and greens like the Mirrie Dancers in the skies.

I uncovered Angus's flask from my cloak and tied a string around it before lowering it into the spring. I let it sink into the depths, and there was a glug of bubbles as it filled. The lights within glowed even brighter, and I could almost see my gaunt face reflected in it. Except, when I looked closer, my eyes blurred together until I only had one.

'Pray sister, what mischief are you planning?'

I nearly jumped from my skin. I turned, searching in the darkness for the source of my brother's voice. He stepped out from the shadows, and the spring's light caught on his antlers like silver. He would have looked menacing to all but me. 'Stop lurking, Cernun. You look like a demon.'

'Maybe I want to look like a demon,' he said. 'What are you doing with that flask?'

I smiled in an attempt to hide my annoyance at being caught. 'What does it look like?' I pulled it from the water as quickly as I could but took care not to let a single drop fall. I needed every last bit if my plan was going to work. The stopper in place, I pulled it under my cloak again and made to leave.

Cernun moved closer to me. 'Nothing from the under-realm besides Callie's own goblet may touch the spring,' he observed.

'Ah. But this is a mortal's flask. It is not from the under-realm.'

His eyes narrowed. 'How in all the realms did you get a mortal's flask?'

'You are not the only one with the wiles of the gods.'

'I'm flattered you think I have wiles.'

'Don't let it go to your head,' I said dryly and turned to leave. But Cernun stepped in front of me.

'What are you going to do with it exactly?'

'None of your business, brother.'

'I hope you're not planning on putting your faith in whichever mortal gave you that.' His mouth contorted into a cunning smile. 'Don't you remember, you should never trust a mortal.'

'You'll forgive me for not trusting your judgement. Your association with them isn't exactly customary.' I pushed him aside and walked towards the corridor.

'It won't work.'

His tone made me hesitate. But if I told him my full plan, he could go to our mother and ruin everything. 'What won't work?'

'Whatever you have planned.' So he didn't know everything. 'It never works. You are not cunning enough, sister. And even if it does work, and you manage to escape with a mortal, things will only end as they did before.'

I turned to face him, staring him down. I noticed he was wearing a second fur cloak about his shoulders, and it gave me a spiteful sense of justice. Let him be cold. Let him rot here while I gain my freedom. 'You underestimate my resolve.'

He grinned and his black coal-like eyes widened. 'Then come, there is no harm in telling me what trick you plan to conjure?'

'And let you use this as leverage to gain favour with mother?' I stepped closer to him, my hands clenched. 'No matter what you say, you know she won't grant you full freedom, not until all of your bloodline are gone from the world. And we both know that will take some time.'

His face twisted and the next words he spoke came out in a hiss. 'Careful Brida, you're playing with fire here.'

'That's the plan.'

~

I barely slept that night and awoke long before dawn. It was time to check on my mother. I climbed the gruelling ascent to the mountaintop, navigating the darkness of the sloping corridors. She was sat on her stone throne surrounded by wisps of cloud, her shoulders hunched, hair billowing in the cool breeze. Her eye was, as I'd expected, closed in a trance. She would be deep in her Sight, pushing her power to shape mountains and rivers and everything in-between. The pale pre-dawn moon shone upon her body, and she looked ethereal, like she could drift up with the clouds at any moment and disappear in a wisp of blue smoke. But her body remained still, only her shallow breaths pushing her chest out proof of life. Even when I prodded her knee, she did not stir. Her Sight was a gradual thing and that made her vulnerable in a way—she could travel miles and miles in her mind, but the further she went, the longer it would take her to return to her physical present.

I left her, but I was still unsettled. I had some time before dawn, so I ventured to the spring. It had been a while since I'd attempted to enter the Sight of my mother. It always left me with a chill and ache in my bones, but I needed to see what she was seeing, how far her mind was, how long it would take for her to be wrenched back if she realised there was a disturbance in the usually quiet under-realm.

Entering it now, I could know for sure that I had the time I needed to escape—to leave the mountain for good without her finding a way to draw me back. And I had learned to use a conduit for my own Sight—water—which sped up the process of returning, although, it prevented me from actually physically interacting with the world or influencing its subjects—only my mother had that ability. I would arrive distant and elusive in a subject's mind, only able to see what they were seeing, and speak to them if I wished.

I leaned over the side of the spring and looked into the depths of the swirling water. I imagined it reflecting more than just a blur of colours. Eventually, a strange ripple began, whether literal or in my mind I never really knew, but I saw it nonetheless and there I was, gripped within Callie's spring and her mind. There was a grey dullness first, a haze. And then images flickered into being. I smiled.

She was soaring above the clouds, in animal form perhaps, a bird—yes, a golden eagle—surveying the land beyond. But it was impossible to tell where she was. With a lurch, I let the Sight pull me in. I held my breath, slowed my heart, cleared my thoughts. My intrusion in my mother's mind had to go unseen for now at least. My outings with my brother had given me enough practice, although he was more used to it, and I rarely liked to push into his mind. It was easier if the subject was willing after all. But I was stealing a connection now, drifting through the clouds, talons beneath me. The golden eagle suddenly dove, down and down together, and it took all I had not to gasp out. The fall made the landscape blur, and then a screech. A tug, and the Sight shifted. In a nearby woods, a doe snuffled and moved. My head spun, and then we were with it instead. It was calm, placid, and I could smell the scent of the dew-damp woods around it. I longed to be there in the flesh, to feel the effect entirely like my mother did. Wildflowers were dotted all around, bluebells and snowdrops, an early sign of spring. Wild garlic brushed along the feet of the doe as she moved to and fro. I tried to push myself out a little, to get a view of the surroundings. It was like letting out a slow breath, the space around me expanding. It was a risk, but I needed a better view. I didn't recognise the surroundings immediately. Cernun had told me stories of the kingdoms beyond our home, of grand castles, flourishing villages, vibrant festivals, lochs and rivers stretching all the way to the sea. My three days of freedom was never long enough to get that far, so I often dreamt of making it to the coast, to swim in the cool waters and look out across an endless horizon.

The doe twisted its head and looked into the distance. There it was, a vast blueness signalling the coast. My mother was at least three days away, and if she were to come back it would take her longer than my own escape, if all went to plan.

I let out my breath slow and steady and pulled myself back into the cavern. The spring lay below me, back to its glimmering form. Outside, a slant of light entered the cavern from the viewpoint gap. Dawn had arrived. I ran over to the gap in the rocks and heard the splash of oars. Angus was here, like he'd promised. And my brother had told me to never to trust a mortal. I could almost taste the freedom in the air as I headed towards the waterfall cave at the base of the mountain. It was time.

It was cold down in the cave, but I didn't start the embers this time. I needed to conserve my energy. Angus was already on the rocks by the waterfall and, when he saw me approach, he waded into the water and stepped under the waterfall to greet me. The water crashed over him, reflecting the sun, briefly shrouding him in a cape and crown of light.

His eyes widened as he took me in again. 'Goddess Brida, you are even more beautiful to behold than I remembered.'

It had only been a day, but I enjoyed the idea that his thoughts had been consumed by me, and only me. 'I wasn't sure you were going to come—that you would keep your promise.'

He chuckled softly then placed his hands on my shoulders, looking upon me like I was made of gold. 'I wouldn't have missed it for the world. Now tell me your plan. What would you have me do?'

I reached into my cloak, took out the flask and handed it to him carefully. 'Take this. It contains water that is very valuable, so you must be careful,' I told him. 'As soon as I come out from under the waterfall, you must douse me in the water from it, using every last drop.'

He nodded, taking hold of the flask, handling it gently. 'Yes. I can do that.'

'This is important,' I said. 'I need you to not be afraid of me. I will look hideous.'

Angus scoffed. 'That is impossible. You are the most beautiful creature I have ever laid eyes upon.'

'For a time, I won't be.' I tried to push back the feeling in my stomach that was bubbling, imagining the pain of what I was about to do. 'But I will be whole once again if you do as I ask.'

He took my hand with his free one and looked deep into my eyes. 'Of course, you can trust me,' he said. And I believed that I could.

'Then I'll see you on the other side,' I said, passing him my pack to take beyond the waterfall. He stepped back through the small channel, and I watched as he stood on the other side of the water, half submerged in the pool beneath the waterfall. His shoulders shook from the cold, but he didn't complain. Soon I'd be there with him, by his side. Free. I stepped so that I stood almost beneath the waterfall, water up to my knees. I tested pushing through it, but it would not let me pass.

*My flesh and skin will not contain me*, I thought. This had to work.

I closed my eyes and held my hands across my chest. Then I took in a long deep breath and held it. As I let it out, I summoned all my energy—every ounce that I had saved over the years—and siphoned the power to my body. I ignited like a cinderblock. My clothes burned first, then it reached my flesh. I couldn't help but scream at the heat of it. Water hissed around me, creating a veil of smoke and steam. I couldn't breathe. The pain was immense, torturous, and I questioned—perhaps too late—if I really was immortal, if there were limits to my power. But I kept the burning going. My skin blistered and bubbled until it was gone entirely, melting away like wax from a candle. My ears were ringing, and I was distantly aware that I might have been screaming. Time moved too slowly, but once my power had been used up, I finally took the first step on flayed skeletal legs, barely taking my weight. As the waterfall crashed over my body, the water stung painfully into every damaged part of me.

But I was on the other side. I'd made it. For a heartbeat, I was aware of the early spring sun, bright as quartz in the sky. Then I tumbled into the pool. The pain was too much.

Everything turned dark, but there was a voice somewhere distant, then hands lifting me up. The voice of my mother rang in my head once more: *May Brida, daughter of Callie, of fire and water, be banished to the under-realm, contained by her flesh and skin, so that she may only pass from the mountain at the turn of the season, when her power may bless the world anew.*

As everything faded, I wondered if I would ever wake up, if my freedom had cost me my life.

# PART TWO

Somewhere nearby a river babbled, wood creaked, and there was a distant swish of a sail. A light breeze tickled my cheeks. For a moment I dwelled in the feeling of it, imagining I was out at sea with Alder long before the curse, exploring the vast ocean and feeling like our love was the most powerful thing in the world. But the memory dissolved as soon as I opened my eyes. There was blue sky, and the sun was high and bright above.

I pushed myself up to a seated position. I was awake, free, away from the under-realm. My woven blanket and Angus's fur cloak had been laid over me, yet still I felt a chill across my entire body, like I'd been drawn out and stretched. But I looked at my hands and there were no sign of burns or marks. My flesh and skin had healed.

On seeing me awake, Angus let the sail drop and the boat slowed. He then rushed towards me as we drifted along the river, surrounded by evergreen trees on either side.

'Brida, my goddess, you are awake.'

I blinked up at him. 'Where are we?'

'On our way home,' he said, then looked me up and down as though afraid I may rise up and curse him. 'I'm taking you to be healed.'

Healed? 'But…the water from the flask, from Callie's spring, did you–'

'Yes…' his voice stuttered, and he avoided eye contact. 'But…it didn't fully work.'

'I don't understand.'

'There was only enough for the top half of your body. Your legs, they're healing but they are…' He paused and shook his head. 'I'm sorry.'

'What?' I asked him sharply.

His voice lowered. 'You should look for yourself. I'm going to check the sails.' Without another look at me, he swept back to the sails, his footsteps clunking heavily.

I turned my attention to my legs and carefully lifted the blanket from me. The bare flesh was wrinkled and dappled, with a raw redness to the skin. Bile rose in my throat. I tried to wiggle my toes. But the movement made it feel like I was burning all over again. I glanced towards Angus. He looked different. His stance was upright, and he had grown taller, muscles rippling under his clothes, hair shining luminescent in the light of the sun. Even his skin was smooth and glowing. And I realised.

'You drank from it?'

Angus still avoided my gaze—he grunted. 'What? Of course not. I would never do such a thing. Why would I betray you?'

Anger rose within me. How dare he do this to me? 'You're lying. Gods, how could I have been so stupid? Of course you betrayed me. I should have listened to my brother.'

He had the audacity to laugh, as if this was all a joke. As if he hadn't just stolen my freedom from me once again. 'Come, Goddess Brida, daughter of Callie, why would I lie to *you*? I did what you asked.' He came closer to me and finally met my eye. I could see the deceit in them and realised it had always been there—this was no noble man, no kindly prince. This was a cruel mortal who had tricked a goddess. I'd been stupid, reckless. I thought of my mother and how much I hated her for driving me to such desperation, to want so badly just a bit of freedom that I eagerly trusted the first mortal I came across.

'You will pay for this, Angus,' I said.

But my words seemed to mean nothing to him, and he continued with the lie. 'You're wrong. Something must have gone wrong with…whatever spell you cast upon that water,' he said. 'But still, I'll take you home and you'll be safe there. Isn't that what you wanted, to come home with me, to get away from your mother? We'll fix it. We will, together. I promise.'

I pursed my lips together. I knew my legs would heal eventually, but now he had taken the water of the under-realm gods. No more was he a mere mortal, but a mortal mind so suddenly in a god's flesh—it was only a recipe for disaster. I had underestimated him, and now I would pay the price. But eventually, he would pay for it too. 'Yes Angus. We will fix it.'

~

We sailed for two days, and Angus was both distant and suffocatingly attentive for every part of the journey. He fussed over my blankets, brought me food and water, gave me a single pale dress to wear for my clothes had burned in my ritual, but he still would not look at me properly. If he brushed my skin or accidentally caught my eye, he rushed away as if he was afraid I may still have some power left to smite him.

I wished that I did. I wished that I had the power to set fire to the boat and drown us both. It would be unpleasant for me, but waking up after the fact, still alive and breathing while he lay at the bottom of the water would have been satisfying enough to endure the pain of dying and the subsequent agony of resurrection.

I looked at Angus, the man I had thought I'd felt something for. But there was nothing there in my heart—just a twist of guilt and a bubbling of shame and anger.

It wasn't like I hadn't been in love before—I should have known that this wasn't the start of it, not even close. I thought of Alder again—of true love when I'd walked the land more freely, before Callie's curse. He was a mortal, and I was a god, but still we were happy for a time. I never wanted to lose him. But fate had other plans. I could still remember the blank look on his face as he plunged from the cliff on that tragic day, taken in by the dark abyss below. Maybe, like gaining my freedom, I was never supposed to be in love.

The river led us further and further away from my home. It twisted and meandered until I could see a vastness of blue ahead. I was finally at the coast, the glistening waves and freshness of the air just within my grasp—but as we reached the openness of water, we only sped along below cliffs and rocks, and my experience of the magic on the open water was short-lived. A town loomed ahead, walled in and dominated by a castle high upon a distant hill. Compared to the claustrophobic dankness of my home, the sight of it sent a slight involuntary thrill through me.

We pulled up at a small bustling harbour at the edge of town and the smell of fish and smoke filled my nostrils. Angus barked orders at the men on the docks, while nervous looks of townspeople fell upon me in my feeble state. I covered my legs with my blanket as best I could and turned away to look out to sea, wishing I could be out there instead— free and unbroken. And away from the whispers of mortals. There was a sound of horses and I turned to see a carriage approaching, grander than anything on the docks. It must belong to Angus. The varnished wood was painted green with a sigil on its side formed of an axe and a boat. Angus appeared hurriedly and lifted me from the boat with ease. He then shoved me inside the dark carriage, closing the door behind without so much as a word. Angus rode up front and I was alone again.

My legs felt numb, and my body ached. From the small window, I watched as cobbled streets glided by, past rows of wooden and stone buildings. More curious looks followed us and there was a clamour of excitement as the townspeople heralded the return of their prince. Had they already noticed he had changed? Did they wonder what strange woman he had brought back from his travels? From the suspicious looks I'd received on the docks, I guessed I would not necessarily be welcomed.

As we entered the castle walls, and the gates closed behind with an echoing thud, the carriage slowed and stopped. Angus came to the door. I told him that I could walk, even though I knew I would fall as soon as I put weight on my legs, but it would have been better than the indignity of being presented in the way that I was—like a maiden in distress. But he ignored my protests and lifted me again as if I was the weight of a feather. A line of guards clad in leather armour, axes tied to their sides, accompanied us towards the castle entrance. Some of them stole a glance at my form, looking me up and down with the same hungry eyes Angus had first gazed upon me with. When my blanket slipped and uncovered part of my bare burned legs, one of them recoiled and cast his eyes away. I looked up to the sky and tried to summon a spark, an ember, anything into my hands, my body. Nothing worked. My power was spent.

Inside, Angus presented me to his father, the King, like I was a sacrificial offering.

'Father, here is Brida, daughter of Callie,' he said, his voice echoing in the high walls of the castle. 'I have rescued her from the under-realm, and so she will live here, with me.'

The King was slumped lazily upon his throne, and I couldn't help but contrast him to my mother. He had none of her grace and stature—just brutishness and a rough edge to every feature. He leaned forward to get a better look at me, then shook his head. 'This is a bad omen,' he said, turning to Angus, nostrils flared. 'What were you thinking of to bring her here? Have you no sense? We will be punished by the Gods for your insolence, boy.'

Angus's grip tightened on my body, and I had to suck in a breath to prevent myself from crying out in pain. Not the venerated prince he had presented himself as after all. It would have made me happier if not for the disgusted look his father now gave me—as if he'd sooner set me on fire than spend another second in my company. The feeling at least was mutual.

'She will be my responsibility,' Angus said. 'I saved her and so she is mine.' I opened my mouth to speak, but Angus spoke loudly so I didn't have the chance to protest that he was wrong, that all he had done was wrong. 'I promise this will bring riches to our land, you will see, father.'

His father's eyes burned with anger. 'She will be kept under lock and key,' he said. 'You will ensure she is fed and watered.' Like I was some pet.

'Until she is better?' Angus said.

He nodded, a sharp nod. 'Then you will return her to the mountain where she belongs. We will not harbour a curse like this here.'

Angus's whole body stiffened, and there was a long silence. 'Yes, of course father,' he said finally. 'Whatever the *King* decrees shall be done.'

And with that, Angus carried me from the throne room, up a spiral windowless tower to my very own chambers in the highest reaches of the castle. The room, at least, had a balcony. Part of me was tempted to crawl over to it and fling myself from it as soon as Angus put me down—though it would only cause pain, and I would awake once again, even more frail than before. It would be a statement however—maybe it would get the townspeople to pay attention. I looked at the open space. Or it would get me iron bars across the whole balcony. I'd bide my time. Better to have an escape route for later.

Angus placed me gently on the four-poster bed which was covered in blankets of scratchy wool and fur. He fussed over me, pulling the blankets around me even when I tried to kick him off. 'I will see to it that you will be looked after, my goddess,' he told me. 'We will get you better, then we will rule this place together.'

'What about your father?' I asked him.

He turned, and a glint of fire reflected in his eyes from the hearth in the corner of the room. 'I will speak to him. Make him see sense,' he said. He placed my pack with my sparse belongings on a table in the corner, then he swept out the room. There was a clunk of a lock behind. From one prison to another.

~

The next day, they came to bathe me. The journey had left me aching, and my skin coated in salty air and water. Servants spent the morning carrying steaming jug after jug filling the wooden tub in the corner of the room. While I yearned for the soothing water, the indignity of it was too much.

When a guard tried to carry me to the bath, I hissed at them.

One of the servants stepped back. 'My...lady, goddess, Brida, we are to help you bathe. It is part of our jobs. Even the King and Prince-'

'You will do no such thing,' I told them. 'Help me stand, then I will undress and bathe myself.'

The servant hesitated, staring between the guard and me, then she nodded to the guard. He gripped my arm tightly while I attempted to stand, but my legs were too weak. They buckled and I fell.

The servants gasped and came to my aid, but I waved them away. The air in the room was thick with rot, like I was dead already in this miserable place. My dress had fallen above my knees and the guard's eyes tracked from my thighs to my ankles—but there was no desire there. Then he cleared his throat and said, 'we have our orders,' and he reached down and lifted me without ceremony. Though I struggled and strained, beating at his chest with my fists, he dumped me still clothed in the searing water, then marched out of the room. I screamed out in pain as the hot water stung into my legs. The pale dress Angus had clad me in ballooned in the water, moving with far more grace than the rest of me. One of the servants leaned in to help me take it off, while the other reached for my arms, a cloth in her hands. 'Get out! Get out or I'll curse you,' I yelled at them.

They didn't need another telling and both scurried away.

Alone and shaking, my body slowly accustomed to the water and the stinging gradually lessened, though never entirely disappeared. My burns were still tender and raw. Steam filled the cold room. Humiliation and rage tugged at me, no good combination for anyone, never mind a deity. I took a slow breath and sank into the bath until I was fully submerged. The muted sound under the water was comforting, and if I focused hard enough, I could almost be back in the under-realm again listening to the battering of a storm through thick rock walls. I opened my eyes and looked up at the blurred, rippling surface, blowing bubbles upwards through my nose. I thought of my mother and tried to summon the Sight. I strained my mind, imagined the images upon the surface. I don't know how long I tried, nor for how long I was under the water, but suddenly across the surface there was a deep orange. The bath water was on fire, flames flickering. And then a sudden darkness, and in it I thought I was flying above the land in the form of a seabird, looking down upon an endless dark sea. Two hands gripped me, and the vision was shattered. I was lifted and wrapped in the bedsheets they'd used to smother the fire. The guard held me in his arms.

'She tried to drown herself. And to burn the whole place down with her!' one of the servants yelled through tears.

And then Angus was there, his eyes flashing across the scene. He took me in, my near nakedness, my body shrouded only in the thin sheet which stuck to every curve of my fragile flesh. He grabbed me from the guard and ordered everyone to leave, then he made to dry and dress me. I had no energy to protest nor feel discomfort at my vulnerability. He said nothing as he worked, and then set me back where I had lain before with a new pale dress and my hair sodden and tangled loose over my shoulders. He stared at me for a long time after, sat in a chair next to my bed, and I stared back.

'You will be more gracious of our hospitality,' he said in a low voice. 'We are only trying to help.'

I jutted my chin out. 'By locking me up under the order of your King?'

He frowned. 'What would you have me do?'

I thought about it. What did I want? I wanted to be healed, I wanted my power back—but could he really give it to me? I could remain locked up here until I got better or end up back in the under-realm to be cursed once again by my mother. And Angus couldn't transfer his power to me…unless? *No.* That's what led to my imprisonment in the first place. To attempt the Sight while so vulnerable would be foolish anyway—so I'd wait. I'd become good at waiting, and my power would surely return. After all, although it had just come unbidden, my power of fire and water still remained. 'You're the mighty Prince of this land, so I will leave it to you to figure out,' I said. 'Or perhaps it is really your father that holds the power here?'

His mouth quivered and he stood up, then marched out the room. And I felt satisfied that I'd got the last word—and that my words still had the power to influence a mortal's mind.

~

Angus didn't visit me for days after our argument. Servants came in and brought me food, water, and ale, though they, at least, didn't attempt to bathe me again. Healers were sent to treat my legs with a strange and sugary concoction that had the texture of milk but the smell of rotting meat. They plugged their noses with hemp but did not offer me such a courtesy. Nor did they really even look or talk to me. If I moved my legs, they'd jump back in fear. If I dared to speak a word, they pretended they hadn't heard me. Maybe they thought that I would curse them. That I was a bad omen like the King had said. Maybe they were right.

Most mornings, I would pass the time sitting in a chair by the balcony—I asked the servants to put me there after I woke, so that I could at least sit and look out across the town rather than be entirely bedridden. I enjoyed the little balcony in its way, to be able to watch the bustling of the courtyard of the castle below and the ant-like movements of the townspeople in the streets beyond. On a haar-free day, I could even see the sea in the distance. I had learned a few things in my observations—that the King was accompanied by a cohort of guards every time he moved through the courtyard below, that he often visited the townspeople, and that Angus did not. Angus moved alone like a shadow on his wanderings, sometimes following his father at a distance, other times going in the opposite direction. I saw him once with one of the servants in the corner of the courtyard, his hands on her, whispering into her ear. At this point I could not feel surprised that his desire had not been for me alone—I had only been a prize for him, and as soon as he had an opportunity for more power, he'd taken it without hesitation.

One afternoon a bard arrived to entertain the King in the courtyard, and I was looking forward to something different. It had been a long time since I'd heard music—Cernun used to play beautifully on the harp before his imprisonment, but he later refused, saying his fingers were too cold to pluck the strings. My mother took away so much enjoyment from life.

The bard waited, not daring to begin until the King and his royal entourage arrived. A select group of townspeople were gathered just behind the cordoned-off archway to hear the performance and to see the King—beloved as he was. Angus was sat lazily in a dark corner, and I thought that he was glancing up at me, though I could not see the direction of gaze for the cloak of his hood had been lifted over his face.

Then there was a yell. Angus stood up and immediately made towards the source of the cry. A servant was running towards the courtyard. The same woman I'd seen Angus with just the week before. She had blood on her arms and down her dress, and a knife in her hand. The townspeople craned for a better look as Angus strode towards her. 'The King,' she shouted. 'He's dead. Prince Angus, you must come at once, you-'

Angus took one look at the servant and pushed her away. 'Murderer!' he yelled. 'She has murdered the King, seize her!'

Guards appeared instantly before the woman could protest, but I saw the look she gave Angus—betrayal, hurt, pain, and something else:

heartbreak. This was clearly not how she'd expected the events to unfold. And it all seemed too easy from here—like it had all been set up. Maybe it had.

Shouts and mutterings echoed through the courtyard in a ripple of shock and accusations, people already pointing their fingers towards the woman that I knew was innocent. And as she was swept away by the guards, Angus looked straight up towards my balcony and nodded his head. This time I could see his expression—and his smile. He had done this for me.

~

A long series of funeral bells rang that afternoon through the town, seven long mournful chimes, over and over again in intervals. Later in the evening, Angus appeared, already wearing the crown of his father. He sat at my side. I recoiled as he reached to touch my hand.

'Are you well, my goddess?'

'I am not yours.'

He tilted his head and smiled, though the expression wasn't reflected in his eyes. 'I suppose you know already that my father is dead. You do not need to fear him anymore. He cannot cast you out now.'

I paused, certain then that he had plotted to kill his father to take the throne. 'It was never him that I feared,' I replied. 'I suppose you set it all up so that the servant would take the blame for it. What did that poor woman ever do to deserve the sentence you've now secured upon her head?'

'You know nothing of what you speak…what I have done for you.'

'I know who you are Angus.'

He blinked at me, confusion sweeping across his face. 'This is…what you accuse, it is… treason.'

'You would know.'

Angus's jaw hardened. 'I have only done as you asked, goddess. I freed you from your prison. And now I… it was all for you!' his voice was rising, and he stood up and began to pace the room. He made to put his head in his hands, but then instantly pulled them back at the touch of the crown, like he was surprised it was there. His hands trembled as he held them in front of his face, staring at them in the dim candlelight of the room. 'You will be healed,' he said more calmly. 'Then you will be happy, here with me. We will be happy together. It will all have been worth it.'

I didn't reply. My silence enraged him even more and he hit his fists against the door so hard I felt the floors vibrate. Then, finally quietened, he walked over to the empty hearth and stared at it for a long time. His shoulders moved as he sobbed. Murder does things to the mind—I knew it would eat away at his soul, that the regret of what he had done would soon be all he could think of. That would be his burden to bear, for eternity now that he was immortal. But I could at least use his guilt to my advantage.

I pushed myself up into a seated position and looked towards the hearth too, the thing that had started this entire ordeal. Maybe it could help end it too. 'I'm sorry Angus,' I said finally. 'I'll try harder, this is just… an adjustment. I'm grateful for what you have done to help me.'

He turned towards me, his body slack and hunched. 'You are my Goddess,' he said. 'I know you saw me with another woman. It was not my intention to upset you. I am ashamed of my association with… a murderer.' He said the words as if he believed them himself. 'I only want you.'

*And my power.* 'Will you do something for me then, my King?' I asked slowly.

He smiled weakly and nodded. 'Anything.'

'I am cold,' I said, clutching my arms around my body. 'Please, could you bring fuel for the fire, have the servants keep it burning throughout the day and night?'

'Of course.'

'And I would so love to try walking again,' I said. 'I would very much like a stick, as I am too weak to do it on my own. Will you do that for me?'

He came and sat next to me, taking my hand in his. I did not push him away this time. 'It is the least I can do, my love.'

It took all of my power not to grimace at his words.

~

After that, Angus hardly visited me, the affairs of his new kingdom taking up most of his time. But the fire did burn endlessly like I'd asked, and gradually I was able to begin to walk with the stick he had a carpenter craft for me—it was fine and sturdy, and I took care to take a few turns around the room each day.

Each morning, after the servants had first stocked the fire anew, I would go over to the hearth and try and draw in some of its power. It took several attempts before I felt the buzz once again in my fingers.

Slowly, I built the power within me, and I would await my moment, my escape. I had waited eternity for my first escape; I could surely manage some months more in this tower. As I was looking out towards the sea one day, I realised with a strange feeling that I even missed my brother. He had been someone to talk to, to confide in, to share in our despair over our mother's actions. Here, I had no one. Just Angus, who seemed gradually to have become frightened to spend too much time with me.

I was no longer enough for him—the novelty of stealing a god had worn off. I did not offer him much encouragement or affection, so perhaps he grew bored. Or perhaps the guilt of murdering his own father had changed him. One day, he came to my chambers to announce he was to leave town and set off on a quest across the sea for new lands, riches and treasure. And so he did.

Over the months, tales of his escapades reached me. A couple of the servants had begun to grow comfortable enough in my company to talk to one another while in my room, and I stayed still and listened.

'I heard he found a land across the sea with so many riches they could not fit it all on one ship,' one said as she applied tonic to my legs, which were now less wrinkled and almost whole again.

The other servant, who was setting the fire in the corner, replied. 'And he's unmatched and undefeated in battle. He must be so strong and smart. It is a shame he is not-' she stopped in her speech immediately and looked towards me, her words caught in her throat.

'It is a shame he is to be away for so long, for the townspeople dearly miss him,' the other woman said, hardly missing a beat and they continued then in silence. I wondered if they thought me a fool, though I did not care what they said or thought of me. I did not want friends here.

Angus's kingdom continued to expand, and his riches swelled, blessed as he was by the power of the Gods. Boats would appear regularly at the harbour, and new people would arrive bringing chests of wares and goods to the castle which was soon full to bursting. I was occasionally brought gifts from him, and though Angus remained on his journeys I received the tokens—a pocket mirror, a golden necklace, a strange red paste that I was told by the servants to use on my lips. I threw them all in the fire and drew the power from them as they burned.

It seemed nowhere was out of reach for Angus. Wherever he set his mind to, he could go, and the waters and rivers would welcome him, mapping outwards until he reached distant oceans and found more land to plunder. He seemed unstoppable.

Until the rains came.

~

The rains were heavy as the leaves turned orange in the second year of my imprisonment. The seasons had been strange to me for a while, stagnant and slippery, as though the weather could not settle on cold, warm, wet or dry. Everything felt off. Even the natural world was confused by it— birds that should have left by autumn remained flitting from building to tree, and when I listened to their song it was like they'd forgotten their own tune. I came to miss my days spent under the mountain. I couldn't have imagined then that escaping there would have led to a life with more despair and even less freedom. At least then I'd have been allowed out for three days. Here, I had begun to forget what the feeling of the earth at my feet was like.

I waited for winter, for the air to cool and the frost to descend. But only more rain arrived, thick and heavy, bringing with it greyness and desperation.

I peered at my water bowl again—maybe I'd be able to use it now. My power had been growing gradually as I absorbed some of the energy from the fire. Even if it would be a risk to be found, to reveal the power I had, I could try and summon the Sight. But who would I go to? Angus, far on distant shores? My mother? But I realised there was one person I longed to speak to. One person who could understand my torment.

I made sure the door was locked and retreated to the furthest and darkest corner of the room. There, I filled the bowl with water from a jug and looked into it. The reflection of my face was gaunt and drawn out, a grey paleness to my skin. My hair was tangled, arranged messily around my face. I fixed it a little before I took a deep breath and let it out slowly, imagining the water moving as I did. Slowly, images swirled like clouds, until the face of my brother came into my mind. For a moment I could see through his eyes. The cold months hadn't yet arrived, so he was still trapped in the under-realm. He sat now in his own chambers, facing the ceiling. I inhaled then exhaled sharply, thinking of my brother's name as I did so. He sat up with a start and for a moment I was disoriented.

'Sister, dearest, where are you?' he asked.

I had never thought I would have been so glad to hear his voice. 'I managed to escape,' I said, wondering if I should tell him my location. Would he tell mother? Would she descend on the castle with all her power? I couldn't decide if I wanted that or not. What I wanted was to escape, to be truly free. 'I have been trapped here too, though.'

I felt his body shift, his muscles tense. 'Mother has been looking for you.'

'Is she angry?'

He paused, thinking about it. 'If she is she isn't showing it,' he said. 'Worried, maybe. But I even think she may be a little impressed.'

'Impressed?'

'Well, you did burn yourself alive on purpose,' he said. 'It was quite unexpected and, frankly, even I am surprised you had it in you. Maybe she is too.'

'Good.'

'Not really,' he said. 'Nothing is good. Not when you've been using your powers for such ill.'

I was confused. 'No,' I whispered. 'I haven't.'

I felt his mind whir, and it took all I had to stay focussed in on him, to not drift away. I could already feel my body ache from the effort. 'You've not been using your powers to change the seasons, the weather?'

'No,' I paused. 'Like I said, I'm trapped here too... I... something happened to me.'

'Did that mortal deceive you after all?' he said, though there was little malice in his voice.

I didn't reply to that, my lack of response confirmation enough. 'Why do you think I'm using my powers for ill?'

'Because, sister,' he said slowly. 'The balance of things has been disturbed. It is all mother talks about when I visit her, although it has been, in a way, a benefit for me because it has not been so cold during my winter months of freedom. But now even that may be at risk, for great floods approach.'

'Floods?'

He closed his eyes, and I saw only darkness. 'Yes. Soon they'll hit the mainland; only those on high ground will be safe.'

*The rains*, I thought.

'A great tragedy has been foreseen,' Cernun continued. 'Unless we return balance to the realm. Our mother thinks you've been trying to manipulate things and that is why the seasons are revolting against her. She thinks you're doing it just to spite her.'

'I haven't been doing anything. I don't even have my...' But I didn't want to admit to Cernun that I'd lost most of my power. 'I *am* innocent,' I finished. Though I realised that was a lie.

'Well then, as innocent and misunderstood as you are, you'll be glad to know she hasn't been able to locate you yet. But when she does, she will bring you back and most likely force you to drink from her spring while in the under-realm, to bind you to its power for good. She won't let you off as lightly as she did the last time.'

'This isn't like the last time, this is different,' I hissed. 'This is because of…' But what was the cause of the rains? What was Angus doing on his trips across the sea? He had the power of the gods now and his greed was driving him—all of this, the rains, the impending flood, was it his fault? Callie always said it only took a little power to shift the balance of things, though I'd always thought that was just her justification for keeping me locked up. That she was exaggerating to instil fear and worry within her kin. 'I need to go and take care of something,' I said. 'It was good to speak to you, brother.'

'Be careful, Brida,' his voice echoed as I let go of my Sight. I returned to the room, and his face shimmered briefly on the water, then disappeared leaving only dark ripples behind.

I felt the familiar ache in my bones that came from stretching my power. This should have been an easy journey—at the height of my power, I could inhabit my brother's mind for a day, or longer. This had been barely minutes. I looked down at my legs and tried to stand without support, but they quaked and buckled. I cried out in frustration. With my walking stick, I stood and hobbled to the hearth where I lay my hands out in front of me, trying to summon the full power of the flames this time. The embers flickered and danced, and they moved to my fingers. The flames weakened and I felt a sudden surge in my body.

With not much time, I reached for the bowl again and thought of Angus. I watched as the surface rippled and moved in waves and then I was seeing through his eyes.

Every part of me hurt this time, like I was burning all over again, but I held on strong. He was on a ship in the middle of the sea, grander than anything I'd seen from the distance by the harbour. A central sail stretched upwards, and the deck was filled with crates and barrels, supplies from his journey abroad. How much of it had he pillaged or plundered? Maybe my mother had been right all along. The crew were merry, laughing away, some with mugs of ale in their hands singing, though their words were muffled. I was in his mind and yet…something was blocking me from hearing it all fully. Like a wall was around his thoughts, trying to keep me out.

*Brida?* he thought.

He knew I was there. I panicked, tried to let go of the Sight, but somehow he held on to me. But he didn't know what he was doing.

He had no control over his powers yet. This feeling felt familiar. Too familiar. It couldn't be happening like this. Not again. I had to get out. I had to–

*Brida,* his words were so clear. *Get out of my head.*

*I...I can't, Angus, you're holding me here. Let me go,* I pleaded.

He yelled out, and my whole body felt contorted and out of place. I could feel his anger burning inside of me, and then he let out a long cry. It echoed violently, sending a pulse across the water. As I looked out from his eyes, waves began, slow at first, but growing, building in surges until they were enormous. The weather had been still, but now a storm battered the ship from all sides.

*Angus!* I tried to get his attention. *Stop!*

But it was too late. He used his power to push me from him, so hard it had quaked the ocean itself. I came back to the room with a shudder. The images of the tidal wave moving away from the ship and the panicked boatmen scurrying around like frightened deer remained imprinted in my mind. And I knew the wave was coming here, towards the castle, towards this town. Our clashing power was pushing the water towards me. My brother's words took on new meaning. A flood was coming. Angus's rage would destroy his own home. I yelled out in pain and frustration and two guards came running in.

'We need to warn everyone,' I shouted.

They looked between one another. 'Goddess Brida,' one said. 'Are you in pain?'

'You'll all die if we stay here,' I said. 'A flood is coming, a great wave. Angus has sent it.'

'Sit down, please,' the guard said. 'We'll get a healer.'

I threw my bowl at him, but he dodged it, and it fell on the floor, splitting into pieces. I felt a brief wrench in my stomach at the loss. 'I don't need a healer,' I said. 'I need you to do as I command and warn your people.'

One of them sighed and stepped towards me, one hand stretched out carefully in front of him, the other on the hilt of his sword. 'Alright, Brida, we'll warn them. Just settle now.'

It took only a single look in their eyes to see they were lying. To see they thought me mad. The raving goddess trapped in her tower while the King galivanted towards distant shores, bringing back riches and fortune. They wouldn't dare hurt me seriously, but nor would they let me go, or trust my words. They were approaching me now, one on either side so that I couldn't run if I tried. Not that I could on my damaged legs. One of them was reaching for something and I spotted a glint of a bottle. 'Here, to settle your nerves,' he said.

'Get away from me!'

But the guard took hold of me. His greasy fingers forced my mouth open—I tried to bite him, but he held my jaw with such force I thought it might break. The other guard then put the bottle to my mouth, pouring the liquid in. An acrid scent filled my mouth and nose and I choked. Though I struggled in their hold, I had no power to resist. I'd used it all inhabiting Angus and my brother's minds. The first guard held his hand over my nose and mouth, and I felt like I was suffocating. Giving in, I swallowed, and the liquid burned into my throat. A tingling sensation spread across my body.

*Curse you all*, I thought as a haze overcame me. *May you all drown.*

I woke abruptly. I was still in my chambers, my mind groggy and distant. A metallic taste filled my mouth. It was dark outside. With a jolt, I heard again what had woken me. Screams. They echoed from the courtyard and town below. I propped myself up to standing with my walking stick and limped over to the balcony. And then I saw it. A dark cloud looming on the horizon moving at pace towards the shore. *No*, not a cloud, but a wave, a giant one that almost blotted out the sky as it grew—the one that Angus had sent.

For a moment I felt a deep sense of pain and guilt as I thought of the hopeless future for the people below, the ones the guards had failed to warn. Yet what had any of them done for me? None had come to my aid. They all knew Angus had me locked in a tower for months on end and they'd turned a blind eye. And now this, and it was their perfect and powerful King's fault—the one who had stolen the power of the gods, the one who had tricked a deity and who had pushed his greed further than he ever should have pushed it.

I could hear the rush of the water approaching. It hit the harbour first with the sound of splitting wood. Then, the buildings. By the time it reached the castle, I had used the last of my strength to pull my body over the balcony. Then, I jumped. As I fell, I thought not of the potential pain I would experience, nor the inevitable discomfort of drowning— but of the aftermath when I would awake and everything around me would be gone. If burning alive couldn't kill me, then I could survive the wave. Then, in a strange act of poetic justice, in the way that fire had freed me, so too would water.

Just before I hit the ground of the courtyard, the tidal wave swept over me, and I was submerged. The weight of it felt like rocks falling upon my body and I struggled to hold my breath as water surged up my nose and into my lungs. The noise was like a roar of thunder, all-encompassing and violent. My vision blurred as shapes rushed past me in the depths. Eventually, the current pulled me back up to the surface and I was being drawn away in violent rapids from the town. I glanced towards it. The castle had been destroyed almost entirely—even my prison tower crumbled behind. The entire town was gone, engulfed by the tidal wave. And I was swept away with it. My body was bruised and battered by debris as the surge took me further and further. I tried not to look at the bodies that moved near me, nor think of the screams of those that had already been tugged away by the currents. I told myself some of the townspeople would make it to safety, to higher ground, or they'd be able to grab hold of pieces of wood until the water eased. The whole scene would remain burned into my mind for a long time. But there was nothing I could have done. Not by then. It was all too late. Soon everything was just a watery abyss, and I faded into darkness.

~

I awoke eventually on a small hillock, as the land drowned around me. I had found myself at last by the ocean, if only by my own folly. I was free and trapped yet again. Even more alone this time. The under-realm, at least, was safe—I could see our mountain loom far away in the distance. The water had not risen quite high enough to reach it.

I waited in the now endless rain, knowing Angus would return to his land one day, to no home, no family, and the goddess he had betrayed.

# PART THREE

I quickly lost track of the days. Part of me had expected my mother to appear, or for her to send Cernun to retrieve me, but neither one came. Maybe this was part of my punishment for the role I'd played in destroying the world. Maybe my crimes were too heinous this time to deserve a place in the under-realm. I would be left to rot here until I was nothing but bones. Would I awake again after that? I had never attempted starvation as a means to escape my imprisonment before.

I huddled upon my lonely rock, thinking of the miserable months that lay behind me. Then my mind drifted to the years before that. I thought again of Alder, when things had seemed so promising.

My mother had forbidden our union at first, but then she allowed it with a warning—for deities could not grow old, mortals could, and she knew that eventually his passing to the afterlife would break me. Deities were not made for love, she told me. Not love of that sort at least. But I was stubborn and still young in the years of the gods.

Had she known that I would try to find a way to save him? That I would search for a cure to his mortality, for a 'cure' to my immortality was impossible, and not something I was sure I even wanted. Not then anyway.

The land in those days was flat and calm, endless meadows and greenery connected to long beaches and oceans where I spent many a night looking up at the sky and tracking constellations. There was no winter or autumn, just long days of sunshine and eternal summer.

The memories of Alder arrived unbidden in my mind while I lay on my hillock of land staring out to sea. The whole ordeal was like a long-forgotten dream. I spoke his name in my mind, imagining he was with me, comforting me as I awaited the other mortal I had pulled under my spell.

We had many long years together. Alder built us a home by the coast and we lived an easy life away from mortals and deities alike. I wove fishing nets and sailed and swam in the crystal still sea. He crafted canoes and sailboats, and we'd go out together until we could no longer see the land, and then we'd pretend that we were the only ones left in the world. I even showed him my Sight—he'd ask me to inhabit the mind of a creature far away on the mainland, or a fish beneath us, then after I'd tell him what I'd seen. I loved the way his eyes lit up as I spoke. I loved how he seemed to drink me in and listen to every word, feel everything I felt. I loved how he shivered on a cold night, and I would have to huddle close to him to stop him from freezing. I loved him. And he loved me.

But nothing so perfect lasts forever. We were out exploring the land one day when there was a tragic accident. Alder was attacked by a wild boar, skewered by tusks that tore into his flesh and skin. He lay there dying in the open land, his face turning grey, tears in his eyes. There was nothing I could do to save him by any mortal means. Then I had an idea—I would inhabit his mind, use my Sight. I had planned to leave a part of me there, a hint of my own power and immortality and in doing so, it would bind us and save his life, for he could use my power to heal. But my Sight was not so refined, nor so skilled back then. Even now I do not have full mastery of it.

At first, I thought it had worked. He survived, healing slowly, but when he returned to physical health, he was a shell of his former self. He walked around indifferent to everything, as though he was blind to the world. He didn't even seem to see me, he just stared through me like I was a ghost. But the worst part was that every so often he would hold his head and scream out, gripped by a sudden madness. On one of his outbursts, I tried to go back into his mind, but it felt different this time. There was a resistance, and he was fighting back against me. The power I'd left there pushed against my own. As I tried to escape it, both of us were flung away from one another with such force I thought I must have been struck by lightning. And then the ground began to shake. As the earth split beneath him, canyons and cliffs formed all around. He looked at me, an intense gaze, like the spell had been lifted and he was finally back to loving me again. I reached out for him, but it was too late. He took one last look at me, smiled, then turned towards the growing gulf of rock and earth and jumped into the endless deep.

My heart broke that day, and so did the world. The fire beneath the earth rose up and earthquakes tore apart the land, leaving our formerly flat, green and beautiful home pockmarked with scars and fissures. Then, some of the new mountains exploded in ash and dust and flumes of fire, pushing land out further and further into the sea that had once belonged to Alder and I. Mountains and ravines, valleys and cliffs wove their way into an uneven landscape. As the ash settled in the atmosphere, the rains came, and then the freeze. The winter was long and unforgiving, and the remaining gods retreated to the under-realm to hide beneath the mountain until it was safe for us once more. When the age of ice ended, mother took her place atop the under-realm on her stone throne and used all her power to quell the storms and bring some balance back, but it tied her to that single spot with her all-seeing eye. She and the land became one, and only through her Sight could she move across it. And me—I was cursed. For my power could do too much damage if allowed to roam free on land. I was to be contained.

Maybe I needed to be contained again. Maybe my mother had been right to curse me. I vowed then, on that hillock as the water surrounded me, that I would learn to control my powers before I used them again. But first, I'd have to right some of the wrongs I had now unleashed.

~

By the time Angus arrived, I had lost my bearing on both time and season, but I remained resolute. The rains had settled a little, and the birds that were left squawked and soared above, circling, wating for me to become carrion. Finally, the sound of a ship approaching came, holding the voices of what was left of Angus's crew, which was less than a dozen men. I looked out towards them. Angus was standing tall upon the deck. When he saw me on the last remaining piece of land, he lowered himself alone into a rowboat and came to me.

Though he still looked strong and powerful, he was seaworn and had lost some of his glow from the day he'd first rescued me. He had clearly been overusing his power and was suffering for it.

'What have you done?' he asked me.

'I have done nothing,' I said. 'This was your doing.'

His nostrils flared. 'No, no, none of this would have happened if not for you!'

'You drank the water of the spring. You took some of our power. But you're too greedy and weak to wield it. Your actions have flooded your home, and you will soon flood the world if you don't stop. Everything is a fine balance. You must end this—give up your greed, use your power for good and we can put the world to rights.'

He scoffed at me. 'You're wrong, I know exactly what I'm doing.'

'Yet here we are. Your home and everything you cared about is gone. Now you must make amends.'

'No.' He began to sound desperate. 'I have only just started my exploring.' He paused and looked towards the mountain, then back to his own ship. 'If everything really is gone here, then I have no reason to stay now. I will go and find new lands, new people to lead. I will leave this land to drown, for it has only brought me misery.'

'And what of me?' I asked him.

'You have only brought me misery too.'

I considered him for a moment, pretended like his words had caused me hurt. 'I'm sorry you see it that way,' I said. 'But so be it. I only have one final favour to ask.'

'I have nothing more to give you.'

'Please, Angus,' I trilled. 'Strong, noble and merciful king with the power of the gods themselves. Please, take me home.  Do not leave me here. I am weak, and I don't wish to be trapped here for the rest of my life.'

His lip twitched, but any desire he once had for me was gone. 'No. Your words no longer affect me. Stay here and rot for all I care.' He turned to leave.

But I'd planned for this. I let out a long and exaggerated breath. 'Then I suppose you will never know what it is like to be a true God…'

He hesitated, his fists balled by his side. 'What do you mean?'

'Well,' I said. 'You did not drink the full dose from Callie's spring.' He turned to face me and I smiled gently. 'If you take me home,' I continued. 'If you do me this last favour, I will get you some of the water so that your power may grow. You will be the strongest King, the strongest God the land has ever seen.'

He shifted, eyes searching my face, trying to find deceit in my expression. I held my gaze and didn't falter. 'You're not going to trick me?'

I shook my head, widened my eyes with innocence. 'No, after everything, I wouldn't dare to cross you. I will fill your flask,' I said. 'And then I will have gone some way to make amends for all the harm I have caused you.'

'And if I do this last favour, you will no longer get in my way?'

I shook my head. 'I will do nothing to stop you from fulfilling your potential. You have my word.'

He gave a sharp nod. 'Then I will take you home, if only to be rid of you forever.'

The ship took us almost all the way to the mountain before the flood began to subside, as if something was driving it away. My mother had already begun her healing of the land. So there was still hope for us yet.

When the vessel could go no further, Angus lifted me into the rowing boat and ordered his men to wait while he took me home. It seemed most of his crew were happy to see me gone, blaming me for the loss of their town. I supposed in a way they had a point. The former King's words had been fulfilled. I wondered what they thought of their new King now—how many of them had lost family because of his actions.

The waterfall appeared eventually, still hiding the cavern safely beyond. I felt cold, a shiver coursing through me as I realised I was about to be entombed beneath the heavy rocks once again. How would my mother punish me this time?

It was almost dusk, and there was an eerie stillness in the air. 'We're here,' he said, pointing towards the waterfall, eyes darting around him. 'Where is this magical water?'

'You must take me up into the under-realm,' I pleaded, looking up at him. 'I am too weak to go alone, so you must help me. I cannot walk there and back myself.'

His face twisted in disgust, but then he let out a huff of breath. 'Fine. Fine.'

Angus jumped into the water, lifted me, then waded towards the waterfall. He didn't even try to shield me as he walked straight under the flow of water.

I half expected Cernun or our mother to appear, but all was quiet.

I pointed to the spiral staircase in the corner. 'There, we must go up there.'

Angus frowned but he did as I asked, and I let him carry me up the spiral staircase. His breath was heavy by the time we reached the cavern. There was no sound of a crackling fire, though there was a small glow in the hearth that illuminated the room just a little—a barely-burning flame to welcome me home.

'Thank you, Angus. You are indeed a merciful and kind king. Please, set me here, by the pool, and I will give you what I promised,' I said. 'If you'll hand me your flask?'

He handed his flask over and I pushed myself up, pretending that each movement brought me great pain, that I was entirely weak and helpless. I dipped the flask in the spring as I had done after we met and filled it carefully. 'That should do it.' I paused. 'But, of course, you must *only* drink from it outside this mountain. That is extremely important. For if you drink it inside your power will become fully that of all the gods in the realms and it will be too much for you to take. It is not for mortals to have such a gift.'

For a second his hand wavered, but he took it with a brief nod. He then stared at me as if he'd had a sudden change of heart—as if he wanted to take me back to be his goddess after all. As if he regretted leaving such a woman as me behind in this grim darkness. The moment passed with his next breath. 'I'm…sorry it had to end this way.'

'As am I.'

He left and headed down the spiral staircase towards the waterfall cave. Slowly, I pushed myself up and hobbled over to the eternal flame. I stood by it and summoned the remaining energy of it into me, until I could stand up straight and walk.

I descended the stairs after Angus, tiptoeing carefully. As I reached the waterfall cave again, there was an almighty yell. I smiled. My plan had worked.

~

'What is the meaning of this?' Angus turned on seeing me approach him. 'You!' Spit escaped his mouth along with the last remnants of the water he'd just drunk from his flask. 'What have you done, witch? Release me now!'

I couldn't help but smile. 'I've done nothing, I told you not to drink the water while in the under-realm.' I glanced at his flask then held my hand to my mouth, savouring the moment. 'You didn't drink it all, did you?'

'How did you...' He spluttered, looking between me and the flask in his hand. He threw it to the ground with such force that it bounced off the floor and into the pool beyond the waterfall. He reached out for it, but his hand hit an invisible barrier. He pulled it back with panic in his eyes. 'You *knew* I would drink it! You tricked me. You will pay for this. I promise you will–'

I let out a long breath. 'What else do I have to lose? You've already destroyed our precious land, and you've squandered my freedom, as you have your own. This is all that you deserve.'

'Why can't I leave? You've cursed me!'

'You wanted to be a God, and the gods are cursed.'

'Reverse it.'

'Only the one who lays a curse may lift it,' I said, relaying the same rules my mother had done to me so many years ago.

'Then go ahead, lift it.'

I stepped towards him, holding onto the wall as I went. 'It was not me who laid the curse.'

He blinked at me. 'What do you mean?'

'It was you. You did this to yourself.'

He started to glance around, flailing with a sudden rage as I'd seen come over him in my chambers in the castle tower. 'Then…I will lift it.'

'Then you must find a way that is beyond your own ego and self-interest, for the water of Callie's spring is bound by a greater good, and to drink from it while within the under-realm is to abide by its laws. Only those with pure intentions may use its power.'

'But you lifted the curse upon you, you found a way.'

'Yes, I found a gap in my mother's curse, for she was not quite exacting enough in her wording,' I smiled. 'You helped me figure that out. I've never thanked you for it. But no matter, for it does not help you now. I lifted my own curse for freedom, to be back in my land where I belonged, not for selfish reasons like your own,' I said to him, my smile faltering a little, remembering I was now back in the under-realm, under my mother's watch. 'But it will be a long time before you find the means to escape, for all you possess is narcissism and vanity.'

A deep laugh came from behind, and Angus and I turned to see my brother skulking down the steps.

Angus almost fell over in fright. 'Demon!'

Cernun laughed. 'Witches and demons, how very predictable for you,' he said, then turned to me, raising an eyebrow. 'Hello sister, I have missed you. But I did warn you to never trust a mortal. It is a shame that mortals are not taught the same about the Gods.'

~

After, I waited in the cave while Angus ran off in a frenzy, perhaps to look for another escape route. I knew better than anyone that there was no hope for that. I then tested the waterfall. My hand slipped under the torrent. Though it still took effort to stand, I could leave if I wanted to—my mother's curse upon me was still broken. I could take Angus's boat, I suddenly realised, flee with the ship. Seeing Angus gone and my power partly returned, would the crew obey me as its captain? No one would deny a vengeful deity's orders, surely?

But I thought then of the balance I had disturbed, of the drowned world that lay before me. Of the promise I'd made while alone on the hillock—that I would never let this happen again. For once was an accident, twice was folly, but for a third offence, I'm not sure I'd be able to defend myself. And what sort of freedom would I have in such a world anyway? Besides, I needed time to heal, to reconnect with my power. I glanced up the mountain, a cloud swirling over its peak. Although there was a risk she may curse me once again, I knew it was time I visited my mother.

~

The top of the mountain was oddly still as I arrived at the peak. My mother sat on her throne, her eye closed. But as soon as I stepped closer, it opened with a creak, and she let out a long sigh in a gust of wind.

She let me stew in the intense silence for a few moments before she spoke. 'I got your letter.'

I held my gaze, even though her direct stare had always unsettled me, like she was looking directly into my soul. Maybe she was. 'You understand why I had to leave?'

She nodded slowly. 'I do. But I see you learned little from your past association with mortals. Look at what you have done to our world.'

'You drove me to this,' I said defiantly. 'This was your fault as much as it was mine.'

She considered that point for a long aching moment, then looked out across the land. I followed her gaze. Floods stretched all the way to the horizon, marked with the occasional mountain or higher ground. I felt a flicker of guilt and regret. Things would never be the same again. Just like the last time I let my powers get the better of me. 'You may be right,' she conceded. 'Have you at least learned your lesson?'

I nodded. 'I will not trust a mortal so readily again.' I took a breath before saying the next words. 'Will you curse me for it?'

But my mother only smiled. 'I'm not sure that would serve any of us well. I have another purpose in mind for you.'

I sucked in a breath. 'Whatever your punishment, I will bear it.'

She laughed. 'Perhaps you have changed,' she said. 'Perhaps shedding your flesh shed some sense of your naivety too. If I had known it were that easy, I might have suggested it to you long ago.'

My skin prickled, but I didn't offer a retort. 'The incident with Alder was an accident. I have paid for it all these long years, but keeping me locked up wasn't the answer.'

'Wasn't it?' she asked. 'If you were not set free, the world would not now be flooded as it is. This will now take much of my energy to fix.'

'Then let me help,' I said. 'I have made the mortal pay for his selfish deeds. He can remain here under the mountain. He has the power of the spring. Maybe in time, when he has accepted his fate, he can serve the under-realm too.'

'I must confess I enjoyed your deceit of that foolish King,' she said. 'And you have shown a commitment that I did not think you capable of, to undergo such pain and torment for your own freedom. I believe you have also learned your lesson of the woes of mortals. So I will offer you a different fate.' She paused and closed her eye. 'You may return to roaming the earth as the seasons change. You will walk the land during Spring and Summer for half the year then return here for Winter when I will take over the task. In that way, we may both conserve our power, and balance will be restored and, eventually, maintained.' She opened her eye and looked down at me again with a warmth I was not used to. 'Maybe my folly was to expect I could do all of this myself, to not offer you a chance of redemption after you first threw our land into disarray. For that, I will grant you this final chance to prove your worth.'

It was more than I could have expected—six months of freedom, to help return the world to how it was. 'I can accept that.'

'Good,' she said. 'But stray from your mission or fall for the greed or wiles of mortals again, and I will not hesitate to end our arrangement.'

'I understand.'

'Then go forth, daughter of the gods, of fire and water. Restore the balance and return our land to rights. Spring has come.'

~

And so the bargain was set. My mother showed a mercy I had not expected—she has not sought to punish me again, though the threat always hangs over me like a storm ready to be summoned if I stray from my path.

The flood waters eventually receded, and now I spend my months of freedom roaming on land, restoring it with life and greenery. I cast my Sight here and there to find where in the wilderness I should venture next.

Birds have begun to sing again, and animals have returned from higher ground to graze and settle amidst the valleys and forests of our land.

Some mortal towns and villages have survived or been rebuilt, and somehow stories have spread of Callie and Brida again when once they had been forgotten: mother and daughter, rulers of the earth. I like that in the stories we are seen as equals. Each Spring, I'm welcomed with altars and offerings, and I visit and walk amongst the mortals without them knowing. I have learned not to reveal my true identity. It is better to have them believe that our power and presence is more elusive, ethereal, that if wronged we could, hypothetically, strike back. It is safer that way, to sustain this view of our power. I enjoy my visits to the festivals, though, especially those of fire where I feel at my most powerful, drawing in the energy of the flames. Afterwards, my power to bless the seasons is bountiful and I will feel a warmth in me that will last the entire year.

Meanwhile, Angus remains embittered in the under-realm. He spends much of his time just staring into Callie's spring, obsessed with his own reflection. He is scared he will one day lose his eternal youth. I have also caught him writing poetry, though every line and verse is about himself or his own torment—it fills me with a certain satisfaction that he has a long way to go before he will be able to break the curse he laid upon himself. I'm not sure if his vanity and arrogance will ever fade. Though all things eventually must come to an end.

With Angus around, Cernun at least has company in the summer months, someone to torment as he did me, though I have noticed that Cernun is now much kinder to me in the Winter when I return. He has perhaps realised that my company compared to Angus is not so bad after all. He even allows me to inhabit his mind regularly, and we roam the lands together in Winter. Through careful practice, I have found a way to transfer some of my warmth to him so that he does not feel the cold so bitterly as he once did. I am learning to control my Sight better, taking care with who, what, and how I use it. Callie is even teaching me some of her own skills of influence, so that we really are becoming one and the same.

Where lands shift and change beneath our gaze, we remain watchful over, beyond and under the mountain—twin goddesses of summer and winter, from day to night and night to day.

# Acknowledgements

Firstly, a huge thank you to Francesca and the Luna Team for putting so much care into this collection, from taking a chance on it to publication. To Jenni Coutts for the stunning cover of my dreams, and Cheney Hewitt for the internal illustrations, making this collection look beautiful inside and out.

This book wouldn't have existed without my love for folklore and fairytales that began from a young age, and was sparked by my parents, and grandparents. To Mum especially, you first let me believe in fairies – we'd leave letters together at the birdfeeder in the garden, and I would always receive handwritten ones and sometimes gifts back (whether they were really from the fairies remains a mystery…!) When we moved to the Highlands when I was ten, I developed even more a love of the sea and the natural world, and while rural living definitely had its challenges, I have fond memories of growing up in such beautiful wilderness. Much of these stories are inspired by these landscapes, the dark and the light.

I may not have kept writing these stories had various editors not taken a chance and first published some of them. So thank you to these magazines and the editors – Elou Carroll of Crow & Cross Keys, Jonathan Maberry for Weird Tales Magazine, Brian Rosten at The Maul Magazine, Anna Madden for Myriad and Dark Matter INK's Monster Lairs, Lori Michelle for Dark Moon Digest, Siobhan and Darragh at Space Cat Press, Elizabeth at Cunning Folk Magazine, JW Stebner for Hexagon Magazine, Noel Chidwick for Shoreline of Infinity and SF Caledonia, Emma Munro and the team at Flash Fiction Online, Steve at Ellipsis Zine, Jonny Syer and the team at Northern Gravy, Damon Barret Roe for Crow's Quill Magazine, Michael at The Great Margin, Shona Kinsella for British Fantasy Society, Seb Reilly at Seaside Gothic, Mark Bilsborough at Wyldblood Press, Signe Maene of Salt & Mirrors & Cats, and Leah, Gillian, Zoë, and the team at Flame Tree Press. Thank you all for first believing in these Scottish folklore tales and for giving me the boost to keep writing them. Literary magazines and anthologies are invaluable and have been so important to me for both building communities, and for growing my love of short stories.

A special thank you also to Chris Gregory at Alternative Stories & Fake Realities for first producing the shorter audio drama version of

Daughter of Fire and Water, which went on to be a finalist in the British Fantasy Awards. Having my work produced in this way really gave me so much confidence in pursuing and sharing these stories. Thank you also to the voice actors who brought the characters to life – Kelsey Griffin, Lewie Watson, Peter Forbes, and Simone Lowe.

In 2020, I was really struggling to find writing motivation in lockdown, so I took Sandra Ireland's course Finding Inspiration from Folklore. It sparked both regular writing practice and some of the stories in this collection, so thank you to Sandra. Also, to Claire Askew and Alice Tarbuck, and Elizabeth Kim for their inspiring courses and writing groups that I also joined online during lockdown.

Thank you to the Scottish Book Trust for the support offered through the New Writers Award in 2020, and to Julie Bertagna, my mentor for that year. This collection, and some of the stories within, were actually linked to a YA novel I was working on with Julie over the mentorship, and she first prompted the idea for the novella Daughter of Fire and Water, by suggesting I explore the back story of one of the characters in it. This led to the audio drama, and now novella, and some of the shared world stories in the collection. So, thank you Julie, for the always thoughtful and insightful feedback, and for encouraging me to delve deeper into the worlds I was creating.

While I wrote most of these stories between 2019-2023, I'm not sure I would have found the time to sit down and weave them all together without the month-long residency at a Scottish castle as part of the Hawthornden Literary Fellowship in 2022 – so thank you to the Hawthornden team, and to my supportive manager at the time Gina Hanrahan, for giving me the time off work to pursue it.

To my early readers – both for the whole collection and some of the stories within – a huge thank you for your considered critique and encouragement: Eris Young, Katalina Watt, Anthea Middleton, Sam Canning, Cecilia Bennett, Annabel Campbell, Lorraine Wilson, C.J Henderson, Dave Goodman, Robbie Guillory, Georgina Love, and my mum Irene Croal. I have to also mention amazingly supportive communities and groups that I'm part of, for writing and beyond: Edinburgh SFF (what would I do without all of you!), the Cymera Fest cohort (shout out to Ann Landmann especially), Scream Team, Funghouls, Hooves and Friends, LFI, and Cosy Club.

And as always, a big thank you to my family for always supporting my writing endeavours, no matter how tetchy I get about the ups and downs – Mum, Dad, and Callum thank you for putting up with my lifelong fantastical whims and dreams!

Finally, thank you to the generous authors who read and blurbed the book – Joanne Harris, Lorraine Wilson, Angie Spoto, Jonathan Maberry, Teika Marija Smits – and to you, the reader, for giving it a chance. I hope you've enjoyed this journey into these dark fantastical worlds.

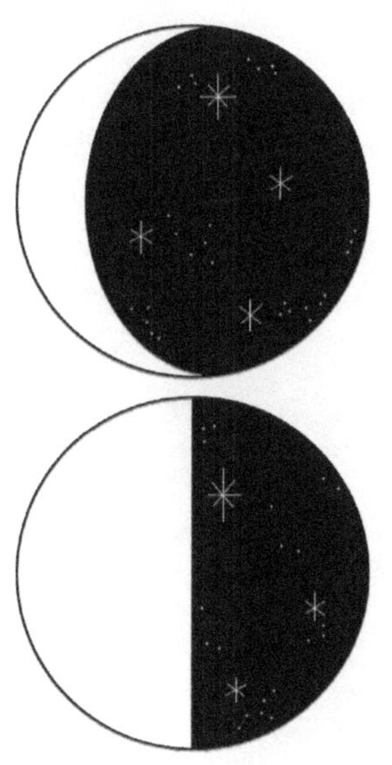

# BONUS SECTION

# Author's Note:

# Finding Inspiration in Scottish Folklore

Growing up in rural Scotland, and often found by the coast, I've always heard tales from Scottish folklore—Selkies, Kelpies, fairies, monsters, and famous hauntings abound. When I first delved into short fiction, I became fascinated in the dark, strange, and rich folklore that Scotland has, from every region. With such an unpredictable climate and seasonal shifts, it's perhaps unsurprising that so many of the folkloric manifestations come with a side of darkness and terror. For example, Scotland has a history of seafaring with treacherous waters, and so there are many creatures and stories explaining why ships might wreck, or why people may be taken by the sea. Dark and deep waters are rife with unexplained phenomenon. That's one of the things I love most about folklore—it has such a close connection to place, that stories can tell us a lot about our local history, politics, culture, or even the natural environment.

While I don't claim to be an academic or expert in everything related to Scottish folklore and Celtic mythology, I have drawn lots of inspiration from researching Scottish folklore and from the tales I grew up with in my writing. A disclaimer that in some of the stories I've very much reimagined the tales more loosely than others, some in more contemporary or even speculative settings. Stories in this collection also took inspiration from Scottish landscape, superstitions, and omens, while others were more directly influenced by stories or creatures from Scottish folklore. With that in mind, below is some brief information about the folkloric inspiration for some of the tales. In the next section, I've also listed sources and books for further reading.

## 'Dark Crescent'—The Sluagh

The Sluagh, or Sluagh Sidhe/'Fairy Host' are spirits of the unforgiven or restless dead. In some stories they were said to move in clouds, while other sources speak of them as winged hosts, moving similarly to a flight of birds, the latter inspiring Dark Crescent. They were said to haunt the night skies, searching for souls to steal and take back to the otherworld.

## 'The Frittening'—The Frittening or The Boneless

The Frittening/The Boneless is a story from Shetland folk tales where a pale, shapeless sea blob was said to have washed up on shore to terrorise the islanders. It would throw itself against windows at night, bring misfortune, steal children, and if you looked too long at it you might lose your mind. Though the creature doesn't appear in its physicality in The Frittening, Sorley certainly believed he could see it.

## 'Nesting'—Magpies, omens, and shapeshifting

For me, seeing a magpie or group of magpies always conjures the rhyme 'one for sorrow, two for joy...' and the superstitions that come with it, like saluting a solitary magpie, or saying good morning to it to scare away bad luck. This was something I'd been told growing up, though there are regional variations to it. Magpies around the world get a bad reputation—even their collective noun is a mischief or, in some areas, a tiding. In Scotland, it was sometimes believed magpies had a drop of the Devil's blood under their tongue, and that if seen near a window death was near. They were also said to be one of the forms that witches could shapeshift into.

## 'Wisp in the Dark'—The Will-o'-the-Wisp

The will-o'-the-wisp most often appears as a spectral light resembling a flickering flame, roving in remote and wild places. It appears mostly at night, occasionally signalling the way to treasure but just as often tempting the unsavvy or weary traveller towards mischief or danger. This may be why it is also known as Ignis Fatuus in Latin, "Foolish Fire". Other names for it include Teine Biorach or "sharp fire" in Scottish Gaelic, or Jack-o'-Lantern in Wales where it is linked to the devil. The latter has become a well-known symbol of Halloween. In the physical form of a carved pumpkin or turnip, the light acts as a guide for those who may go guising on Samhain night, leading children from place to place with tricks or treat in store, just like the will-o'-the-wisp does for travellers when found. It was this intersection that inspired the picnic scene in Wisp in the Dark.

## 'The Taxidermist'—The Cat-Sìth

The Cat-Sìth appeared as a large black ghostlike cat with a tiny white patch on its chest. They walk on all fours, but when not being watched would stand on two legs. One of the theories about them is that they are actually witches who could transform into a cat nine times before the change became permanent, a possible origin of "nine lives". They prowled the streets for souls to steal, which they could do by passing over the corpse of someone dead before burial. They were said to be drawn in by warmth, so in the Scottish Highlands, fires would not be lit near bodies during the wake so as to keep the Cat-Sìth away. It was sometimes said that they could be summoned in a dark ceremony to grant a wish, and around Samhain, houses could leave saucers of milk out so as to be blessed by the Cat-Sìth—those that didn't could be cursed.

## 'Be Still, Iron Heart'—The Ghillie Dhu

In the birch woods by Gairloch in the Scottish Highlands, it was said that the Ghillie Dhu—a tree guardian—wandered here and there, cloaked in leaves and moss. Though he'd often help lost children, he wasn't so kind to adults. I'm particularly fond of this folklore as I grew up in a house called Birchwood in Gairloch, where woodland stretched behind the house, and I found myself thinking of mythical beings lurking in the trees. The Green Man is a common occurrence in British folklore and beyond.

## 'The Fiddler and the Muse'—Baobhan Sith and the Fiddlers of Tomnahurich Hill

The Baobhan Sith is a vampire-like being in Scottish folklore appearing as beautiful woman to trick and seduce her victims. She was said to lure young hunters, dance with them until they were too exhausted to escape, then overpower them and drink their blood. For this tale, I also took some inspiration from Tomnahurich Hill, overlooking Inverness and said to be a fairy hill. Here, two fiddle players fell victim to a trick when they were invited by a mysterious man to play music at a grand party atop the hill, with the promise of gold, fine food, and ale. They played their music until dawn when the mysterious man paid them and bid them farewell. The night of festivities over, they wandered back to Inverness. But everything looked strange—the town and buildings had changed, and even the people were dressed differently. They wandered aimlessly, coming eventually to a church where they found their names engraved on a tombstone. Alarmed, they ran to find the Minister, but on passing the threshold of the Church the gold turned to leaves in their hands, as they themselves turned to dust. The fiddlers had been tricked in the Kingdom of the Fairies, where they had played music for not only one night but 100 years. I first found this tale in a book from the 1800s, and I just loved this idea of time-travelling magic.

## 'Woman of Ravens'—The Cailleach

There are many stories and interpretations of the Cailleach, the Scottish goddess of Winter, also known as Cailleach Bheur or Queen Beira. She is sometimes said to appear as a raven, where a touch might bring death. In the Woman of Ravens, the grey woman was inspired by the Cailleach, though so too was the woman who became at one with the ravens herself. I like to imagine that the Cailleach would have sought to help any who had suffered from the horrific treatment of women in Scotland's witch trials.

## 'Nuckelavee Winter'—The Nuckelavee

The Nuckelavee or "devil of the sea" is one of my favourite, and probably creepiest, creature manifestations in folklore. From Orcadian mythology, it is depicted as a terrifying sea creature, part horse, part man with no skin and black blood. Its breath could cause droughts, spoil crops or bring about a plague. The Nuckelavee is often depicted as at odds with the Sea Mither, who keeps it contained during the summer months. In some stories, the only way to escape its wrath was to step into fresh water, but come across it by the sea at your peril.

## 'Two Faces of Winter'—Bride and the Cailleach

Bride and the Cailleach (or Beira/Cailleach Bheur) are often seen as twin goddesses in various Celtic mythologies—one residing over Winter, the other over Spring. The Cailleach is said to bring the cold months at Samhain by washing her great plaid at Corryvreckan on the west coast of Scotland, a whirlpool or cauldron. The Cailleach in these tales is described as a blue-skinned giant, with a single sharp eye, residing her watch over the Winter months. In Spring she is defeated by opposing Spring forces. In some tales, it is suggested that Bride and the Cailleach are the same person, but she is simply reborn as a young woman in Spring and becomes an old "crone" in Winter. In Two Faces of Winter, I wanted to explore this idea, where the battle for transformation is with herself as the seasons change.

## 'To Gut a Fish, First Gather its Bones'—The Marool

The Marool is a large sea creature from Shetland folklore resembling an anglerfish. With eyes all over its head and a flame crest, it is said to be found glowing phosphorescent in mareel or sea-foam. When ships capsize in stormy weather, it is said the Marool sings with joy at the misfortune.

## 'The Lighthouse Seer'—Selkies

Selkies are one of the most common beings written about from Scottish folklore. I love how they represent an affinity with both land and sea, and a balance to be struck that always demands some element of sacrifice. The Selkie has a grey sealskin coat that can be taken off when walking on land. In some stories, the coat is stolen by humans to trap the Selkie on land, often making them forget their roots to the sea.

## 'A Change in the Rain'—The Frittening, again, and more

While this story was initially inspired by 'The Frittening' phenomenon—with the folklore as mentioned above—it morphed into something more eco-dystopian, with touches of superstition and omens, so I wanted to include both interpretations in the collection.

## 'The Fisherman's Wish'—The Ceasg

The Ceasg is a Scottish mermaid half-woman, half-salmon. In some tales, she swallowed men whole, trapping them in her stomach. To rescue them, her soul—often contained in an enchanted egg—had to be destroyed. If caught, she could also grant wishes to her captor, which inspired the premise of The Fisherman's Wish.

## 'The Woman of Thorns and the Honeycomb Queen'—The Otherworld, Changelings, and Bee-telling

The Otherworld is portrayed as either the land of the faeries/sìth and gods, and sometimes the land of the dead, in Celtic mythology and Gaelic folklore. In Celtic mythology, bees could travel between the worlds, and were often said to be messengers to the spirit realm. There is also a tradition of bee-telling or telling the bees that came from informing the bees that a loved one had died, and it was thought to be bad luck not to tell them of death or a major event. These elements were the initial inspiration for The Woman of Thorns and the Honeycomb Queen, but I also took inspiration from trickster faeries and the Changeling myth— where humans and faeries are swapped at birth, the humans then used for dark purposes.

## 'The Loneliness of Water'—The Sea Mither

The Sea Mither or Mither O' the Sea is mentioned in a few stories in this collection. She is a deity from Orcadian folklore with dominion over the seas and is said to be responsible for calming and warming summer waters. She is often connected to the Nuckelavee too, and could keep the creature at bay during the Summer months, though her power would wane in winter. In The Loneliness of Water, I imagined what she may manifest as in a post-climate change impacted world, becoming the "Sea Witch".

## 'A Kelpie's Breath'—Kelpies and Each Uisge

The Kelpie (found usually in rivers or lochs) and the similar creature Each Uisge (latter usually found by the sea) are shapeshifting creatures that may appear in different forms to lure humans to the water, then drag the victims to watery depths. Usually they are depicted in their horse forms, manes dripping, pondweed or seaweed in their manes, but can disguise themselves as humans.

## 'The Wulver's Gift'—The Wulver

There is some speculation about whether this tale is "false folklore", or more modern than older tales, but still I enjoyed the idea of a benevolent creature which breaks the mould of usual werewolf-type stories. The Wulver from Shetland lore is half-man, half-wolf, and was said to help islanders with gifts such as food for those in need. He was also said to help lost travellers who found themselves waylaid along treacherous island landscapes.

## 'Seedseeker'—Hagstones, Seer Stones and the Otherworld

Part of the inspiration in this story came from finding a hagstone on a beach in Aberdeenshire, sparking the idea for an uncharacteristically for me hopeful tale. Hagstones are stones with natural holes bored in the centre are thought to bring good luck and can be worn for protection and to ward off evil. In tales I heard as a child, it was said you could look through the hole to peek through into the faery or otherworld. The seer stone name came from the idea they can even give a look into the future.

## 'Daughter of Fire and Water'—Bride and Angus, and the Cailleach/Beira

In addition to the folklore mentioned for 'Two Faces of Winter', Daughter of Fire and Water took loose inspiration from the tale as set out by 20th Century folklorist Donald Alexander Mackenzie, particularly the chapter on 'The Coming of Angus and Bride'. In this interpretation, Beira rules harshly over the lands, keeping Bride captive. When she is freed with the help of Angus-the-Ever-Young, Bride brought spring, and Beira the "Ice Hag" fell into a deep sleep until summer and autumn were over and past. 'Daughter of Fire and Water' takes quite a different turn, owed to additional folklore found around the Cailleach and Bride, with shapeshifting, the Corryvreckan whirlpool, and the battle between the seasons.

*Three of the tales in this collection, 'The Constellations of Daughter Death', 'A Song, Remembered', and 'The Last Call of the Deep' don't have specific inspiration from folklore, but are original fairytales inspired in part by Scottish land and seascapes, other worlds, and the idea of seasonal renewal, fitting in with many of the folklore themes and inspiration from other stories in the collection.*

# Bibliography
# & Further Reading

## Books

Breslin, Teresa (2012). *An Illustrated Treasury of Scottish Folk and Fairy Tales*, Floris Books.

Douglas, Ronald Macdonald (1982). *Scottish Lore and Folklore,* Crown Publishers.

George, Douglas (2003). *Scottish Fairy and Folk Tales*, Dover Publications Inc., Illustrated Edition.

Mackenzie, Donald Alexander (1917). *Wonder Tales from Scottish Myth & Legend*, Blackie and Son Ltd.

Monaghan, Patricia (2009). *The Encyclopedia of Celtic Mythology and Folklore*, Infobase Publishing.

Ross, Anne, (1976). *The Folklore of the Scottish Highlands*, Barnes & Noble.

Folk Tales Authors (2019). *The Anthology of Scottish Folk Tales*, The History Press.

Westwood & Kingshill (2011). *The Lore of Scotland: A guide to Scottish legends*, Random House Books.

Winsham, Willow (2022). *Magpies & Red Skies—The Enchanting Origins of 100 Superstitions*, Welbeck.

Winsham, Willow and Chainey, Dee Dee, (2021). *Treasury of Folklore—Seas and Rivers: Sirens, Selkies and Ghost Ships*, Batsford.

## Websites

Cunning Folk Magazine: www.cunning-folk.com
Druidry: www.druidry.org
Folklore Thursday: folklorethursday.com
Icy Sedgwick: www.icysedgwick.com
Orkneyjar: The heritage of the Orkney Islands: www.orkneyjar.com
Signe Maene: www.signemaene.com
Sandra Ireland: www.sandrairelandauthor.com
Tairis: www.tairis.co.uk

## Podcasts

Alternative Stories and Fake Realities
History and Folklore Podcast Myth, Legend & Lore Podcast
Fabulous Folklore with Icy
Folklore, Food and Fairy tales
The Folklore Podcast

# A Note on Daughter of Fire and Water

'Daughter of Fire and Water: A Novella' is adapted and extended from the audio drama by the same title, also written by the author. The audio drama was produced in two episodes by the podcast Alternative Stories & Fake Realities and was a British Fantasy Award Finalist for Best Audio. You can find the full audio drama on all major podcast platforms.

# Content Notes & Warnings

**Dark Crescent:** death of a loved one/grief.
**The Frittening:** implied scenes of animal harm and suicide.
**To Gut a Fish, First Gather its Bones:** death and loss of family member.
**Nesting:** body horror.
**The Fiddler and the Muse:** body horror.
**The Woman of Ravens:** body horror.
**Daughter of Fire and Water:** body horror/injury by fire.